CHAPTER ONE

Cassie Holmes-Smith took the antibacterial wipe running it over her work station, keyboard and desk. She didn't know why HMRC employed cleaners. A duster waved in the general direction of her desk appeared to be the norm and if she should still be at her desk when the cleaner hoovered the underneath of her desk would not get done.

Cassie had already worked through her mental checklist on her 5K morning run. This morning's checklist had been pretty short, work wise, as there was nothing time pressured to be done, unlike other weeks. This week, she didn't need to know which afternoons her boss Alan was on the golf course. She had found there was no point completing time pressured work only to find out that Alan, who she needed to authorise it, was on the first tee.

The local residents' association of which she was chairwoman didn't meet for another two weeks and the carnival committee of which she was treasurer wasn't due to meet for another three weeks, all the same, she had brought the Carnival Committee accounts up to date yesterday.

Her children, Wendy eighteen and Barney sixteen, had what they needed for school today. Which, for

Wendy, meant that she had all she could possibly require for each lesson in today's time table. For Barney, she had ensured he had his sports kit as he had games on a Monday.

Wendy was a high achiever. If she got nine A*s and an A, she would work and work until she got ten A*s. Cassie thought back to when her children were small, Wendy cuddling Barney. Wendy now loathed Barney, his friends and their stupid card games.

Cassie was pleased that Barney had such a close knit group of friends and she was delighted, when they took over her dining room with their games of Yu Gi Oh, their youthful shouts and laughter made her smile although she freely admitted that she didn't understand the game.

'Oh,' she thought to herself, 'that reminds me, I promised to take Barney to a Yu Gi Oh tournament next Saturday'.

Last, but not least, there was Shaun, her husband. Childhood sweethearts, for each other there never had been anyone else. She had already made Shaun's sandwiches.

Cassie was thirty-eight years old. She was five foot seven tall, blonde and she wore her hair tied back off her face, she was naturally attractive and wore very little makeup. As you might imagine from her daily runs she was fit and slim, with what her boss Alan called 'no meat on her bones'.

Cassie had joined Customs and Excise after leaving school. She loved her family and she loved her job. Cassie was always busy, Shaun told her she took on too much, but he knew that was just how Cassie was.

Work wise Cassie's decks were fairly clear as she had worked late last week to finish the issuing of tax assessments on an investigation she had been working. She had written a sixty-five-page VAT assessment letter, plus appendices and a slightly longer explanation letter to the eight years of corporation tax assessments she had issued. Lastly, she had issued penalty explanation letters to the company, advising of the penalties she intended to assess. She would have to wait thirty days before issuing the penalty assessments. This was to give the company the chance to reply regarding the intended penalties. Which the company wouldn't. Cassie would also issue Personal Liability notices to the company directors. Which meant that when the company went into liquidation, which it would, the directors would be personally liable for the penalties which Cassie would assess on the company. This could all of course be appealed and decided by a judge many years later. So, Cassie's objective was to ensure that when the judge read her assessment letters all aspects that the judge wished to consider would be covered by the letter and the appeals would be dismissed.

This certainly was not the norm for HMRC assessments, but it was what Cassie had learned from a very experienced investigator on the team, now retired. He had also stressed, always refer to the statute, establish the facts and apply the statute to those facts. HMRC guidance manuals are just that, guidance, a judge will decide the appeal based on the facts and the statute, so hence the very long letters.

As Cassie had finished the last of the letters on Friday evening, she had thought to herself, 'now get out of that without moving'. This had been what her dad would say to her and her sister when they were kids and he had one of them in an arm lock.

Cassie's dad had had a varied career, of Royal Navy Sailor, a policeman, a publican and a town clerk, all before he was forty-five years old. This provided him with a wealth of stories to share with family and friends that Cassie and her sister had heard many times over. Despite this, the stories never failed to make them smile. Cassie and her sister adored their father. He was a warm, kind man who was always firm but fair, especially during his career as a policeman. Cassie felt that she too was firm but fair in her career as a Fraud Investigator, although she was sure that the taxpayers she investigated did not see her that way.

Cassie's assessments would go out in the post Monday morning to the Trader. Cassie's background was Customs and Excise, where you dealt with Traders. Anyway, Tax payer was a misnomer, for most of the people Alan's team dealt with, and Alan would disown her if she ever used the term Customer. Alan's team was part of HMRC's Fraud Investigation Service, undertaking civil investigation of fraud, under Code of Practice 9.

Under Code of Practice 9, Cassie would write to the Trader to advise them that HMRC had reason to suspect them of tax fraud. If the Trader admitted to the tax fraud and told HMRC all about it, HMRC wouldn't criminally investigate the Trader in respect of the tax fraud to which they had admitted. Criminal investigations would normally mean an early morning Knock with search warrants for the Trader's home and business premises, followed by an interview under caution at a local police station. HMRC's Fraud Investigation Service also carried out investigations under Code of Practice 8, which was a civil investigation without the allegation of tax fraud.

To get back to Cassie's assessments and the appeals against them, there was always the question of the judge on the day. Cassie was familiar with the 2017 judgement in the case of Vowles v HMRC. HMRC had assessed Rebecca Vowles in respect of dividends paid to her by the company, as she was recorded at Companies House as a shareholder in the company. In the penultimate paragraph of the judgement, the judge indicated that HMRC may be surprised by the judgement and advised that HMRC should assess Max Walker, the man with whom Rebecca Vowles had previously been living. Max Walker was not recorded on Companies House records as a shareholder of the company and could not be a director, having been disqualified.

Cassie had vowed to herself that if she ever had a, 'it's not me guv it's him' type case, she would assess them both, and a few years later one came along.

Cassie had inherited the case from an investigator who had moved to London. She didn't particularly like working Code of Practice 9 investigations where she hadn't interviewed the Trader, but that's the way the "Wookie grumbles", as Alan had said when giving her the case. The case concerned a company running a Turkish restaurant in London. The director of the company, Osman, was being investigated under Code of Practice 9. He had accepted the offer under Code of Practice 9 and admitted to tax fraud, but all he had admitted to was £15,000 undeclared tips. HMRC had reason to believe that not all of the turnover from the restaurant had been declared for tax. Criminal Investigations, however, didn't want to take the case over and so it remained a civil investigation.

Despite a meeting with Cassie's predecessor, no further admission of tax fraud had been made. The trader, Osman, had explained at the meeting that the reason the company's turnover was less than HMRC would expect was because, whilst the company ran the ground floor restaurant, the basement was a separate restaurant run by his brother Mehmet.

Cassie began by reading all the case papers, then she started reading the restaurant's 247 Trip Advisor reviews. She looked at each of the photos online and a few YouTube videos which were available. There was absolutely no evidence of there being two restaurants. What was clear was that on the weekends there was music and a belly dancer.

Cassie noticed that Alan had walked past her desk slightly slower than usual when she had a photo of one of the belly dancers on her screen. What Cassie's research showed, aside from photos of belly dancers, was that there were lots of photos of Osman with smiling customers, but only one photo of Mehmet dressed in a colour of chef's jacket no longer worn in the restaurant.
Cassie rang Osman's Tax Adviser and advised him she wanted a meeting with both brothers in the basement restaurant, with whatever professional adviser they both wished to bring. The Tax Adviser said he would arrange this.

Much to Cassie's surprise Osman's tax adviser emailed her to let her know he would also now represent Mehmet as well as Osman and attached to the email were statements for the bank account in Mehmet's name into which the sales for the basement restaurant had been made.

"Now we are getting somewhere", Cassie thought.

After about six weeks of one excuse or another a date for the meeting was agreed. A few days before the meeting Cassie wandered over to Alan's desk and asked, "Can we have a quick chat about my Turkish restaurant case?"

Alan was 63, 5' 9", stocky with a beer gut, but not what you would call fat. Despite his age his hair and moustache were jet black and he always seemed to have a glint in his brown eyes and a grin on his face.

Alan pulled up a chair for Cassie and after sitting down Cassie enquired, "Whichever brother has had the money, what do we do about referral to Criminal Investigations?"

Alan replied, "It's a restaurant case and it's messy. Criminal won't want it. Whichever brother had the money, deal with it civilly." Just what Cassie hoped he would say.

On the day of the meeting Cassie had already done a full day's work before she even got on the morning train. She had got breakfast ready for the children, made packed lunches for them and Shaun, unloaded the dishwasher, put on a wash, fed and walked the dog, checked the kids' school bags, organised drop off and pick up for school, left a note for Shaun telling him where she was going and what time she would be back and put food in the slow cooker for tonight's dinner. After a number of tube journeys from Paddington and after a short walk she arrived at the restaurant. Cassie was hot in her business suit and was pleased to see the large, canopied outdoor dining area at the front of the restaurant as it would offer her relief from the bright sunshine. The business owner's obvious attempt at making the restaurant look classy was let down by the McDonald's-style menu board displayed outside at the front of the restaurant just like the cheap restaurants found in seaside resorts such as Bodrum in Turkey. Cassie stepped inside and recognised the layout from the videos that she had watched on YouTube with the stairs to the basement restaurant on the right hand side of the front doorway. Having introduced herself to a member of staff she was shown to the basement restaurant where two men were waiting. Cassie recognised Osman from the Trip Adviser photos. The other man introduced himself, he was the Tax Adviser that Cassie had been communicating with.

"Where's Mehmet?" Cassi asked.

The Tax advisor advised, "He's a crazy man. He was shouting outside my office last week."
"Just the man to run a busy restaurant," Cassie thought.

Before she could say anything however, a woman marched in. She was wearing typical local Council Official's style workwear of smart but affordable jacket and trousers with a plain shirt underneath. She barked, "Which of you is in charge?"

Osman nervously raised his hand.

"I am from Environmental Health and this is an unannounced visit," the woman said.

Cassie smiled at the woman and explained, "I am from HMRC and it's taken six weeks to arrange this meeting. Is there any chance you could carry out your inspection on another day?"

The woman's face changed instantly to a smile and she replied, "Sure, no problem," recognising a fellow investigator who was on Osman's case whilst she, being local, could happily return any time. After all, it hadn't been a wasted visit because she had enjoyed seeing the colour drain from Osman's face when she announced that she was from Environmental Health.

"When are you coming back?" Osman asked, beads of sweat appearing on his upper lip.

The woman's face had returned to a scowl, "I'm not telling you that," she snarled. Then she turned on her heel and marched out.

Osman ran a finger around his collar feeling hot and uncomfortable.

The Tax Advisor repeated the explanation that Mehmet ran the basement as a separate restaurant. Cassie turned to face Osman whose hands were now clenched into fists, his knuckles turned white. "Here's what's going to happen," she said. "I am going to assess both the Company and Mehmet on the sales paid into the bank account in Mehmet's name. If you disagree you can both go to court and let a Judge decide which of you should be taxed on the undeclared sales. In addition, I am going to charge the Company the highest penalties I can under the circumstances, because you haven't disclosed to HMRC that the monies paid into the bank account in Mehmet's name were undeclared sales made by the company. Based on the Company's last balance sheet, it doesn't have the money to pay the tax I will be assessing, so the Company is insolvent. I will therefore be making you personally liable for those penalties and I am going to start this action tomorrow. Even at this very late stage, there is a chance for you to reduce those penalties by telling me the truth, but time is running out. So do you have anything to tell me?"

The Tax Advisor looked at Cassie in awe, he hadn't expected such an attractive woman to be such a hard ball.

There followed a conversation between Osman and his Tax Advisor in what Cassie assumed was Turkish. Osman's eyes were getting wider and wider as they spoke and the gesticulating got fiercer and fiercer. Eventually the Tax Advisor said to Cassie "Osman has something to tell you." Osman explained that the restaurant had been doing well and he had come under pressure from the family back in Turkey to bring Mehmet into the business. That was why he had opened the bank account in Mehmet's name. The plan was that Mehmet would run the basement as a separate restaurant but, after about ten days, Mehmet had walked out claiming he couldn't cope with the stress.

"When was this?" Cassie asked.

"About five years ago," Osman replied.

"Who controlled the bank account in Mehmet's name?" Cassie queried.

"I did, always," Osman replied. This all fitted in Cassie thought with the date the account had been opened in Mehmet's name and the photo of Mehmet in the old colour of chef's jacket.

"So what happened next?" Cassie asked.

Osman looked a bit not plussed, "He walked out and never came back."

"But he's still on the company payroll," Cassie pointed out.

Osman explained that even after Mehmet had walked out, the family back in Turkey still wanted Osman to financially support Mehmet.

"You haven't been supporting Mehmet, the company has," Cassie explained. Osman now sat leaning forward on his chair, clutching the edge of the table. The Tax Advisor looked relieved that the truth was finally coming out.

Cassie told the Tax Advisor which assessments she would be raising and why. The monies paid into the bank account in Mehmet's name will be used to recalculate the sales for tax, the wages paid to Mehmet after he had left would be disallowed. All of the monies paid out of the account in Mehmet's name would be regarded as monies owed by Osman to the Company giving rise to a charge on the company of 32.5% of the money owed.

"Not all of that money went to me, I paid bands and belly dancers," said Osman, realising that the figures were adding up.

"Do you have documentary evidence of that?" Cassie asked. Osman shook his head.

"Do you have the names, addresses and telephone numbers of these people you paid? So I can contact them and ask them what they got paid by the company?" Cassie queried. Osman had thoughts of an angry belly dancer after being contacted by HMRC and shook his head. Cassie might be scaring him but not as much as an angry belly dancer would.

Cassie looked up and caught sight of her reflection in one of the oversized, gilded mirrors hanging on the restaurant wall. She looked hot, she was on fire! Cassie smoothed her hair with her hand and continued.

"So, as I was saying," trying to keep the smile from her face, "all of that will be liable to a charge. There will of course be interest and penalties and a Personal Liability notice on Osman, making him personally liable for the Company's penalties." She was really enjoying herself now but not so much that she had forgotten to add, "Then of course, there are the tips Osman has admitted to deliberately failing to declare and the tax, interest and penalties he is personally liable to in respect of those tips. I should get the assessment out in the next two weeks. Any questions?" Osman sat there feeling abused by his family and stitched up by HMRC.

Both Osman and his Tax Advisor shook their heads, Osman afraid to speak for fear of getting himself even deeper in trouble. Cassie stood up, collected her things, shook hands with the two men and she said, "Thank you Gentlemen." As she left the restaurant into the full sunlight leaving the dim light of the basement she smiled satisfied at a job well done.

When she got back to the office in Bristol Alan was still there, he had worked late awaiting Cassie's return. Cassie dropped her coat and bag on her desk and then sat down in the chair next to Alan's desk which he had beckoned her to sit in. Smiling broadly Cassie told Alan that Osman had eventually coughed, Alan smiled. Then she told him about the lady from Environmental Health and he chuckled.

"A smile and a chuckle from Alan! High praise indeed," thought Cassie.

"I bet he was delighted when you left," joked Alan.

"A rarity," thought Cassie. A joke from Alan she actually got! Osman's last minute disclosure certainly had been a Turkish delight. She would reward herself for a good job done with a run before getting dinner out of the slow cooker ready for the family that night.

Later in bed lying in Shaun's arms she turned to her husband, kissed him tenderly on the lips and thought, "a run's not the only thing I'm going to reward myself with tonight."

CHAPTER TWO

Cassie had worked bloody hard to be where she was, a Grade 7, Fully Trained Inspector of Taxes. Fully Trained meant she had gone through two years of exams, followed by a year of consolidation where she was required to demonstrate she was able to do the job, by essentially working twice as hard as those who had already fully qualified. If you failed one exam you could retake it. Fail it again and you were off the course. Cassie though had passed all of her exams first time. You could be promoted to Grade 7 by becoming a manager and not passing the Fully Trained inspector course. So, to those who had slogged their way through the exams and the period of consolidation, being a Fully Trained Inspector was important.

On the day that Cassie gained her promotion Alan had said to her, "Well done, if you had bollocks you would have worked them off you have worked so hard."

Some women might have been offended by Alan's comment but Cassie knew he was paying her a massive compliment and she treasured it.

Before joining Alan's team Cassie had cut her teeth on a VAT cash team. This involved visiting a business, often a restaurant, about closing time and requiring the person in charge to cash up the Trader's sales for the night. Often combined with a Test Eat, to check if the meals purchased earlier in the evening, by HMRC staff posing as customers, had been included in that night's takings. Not a job for the faint hearted, but Cassie had thrived on it.

Cassie had worked on Alan's team for fifteen years now. She was thought of as a really good investigator by her older colleagues and her younger colleagues looked up to her.

Under Code of Practice 9 HMRC would ask for an opening meeting with the Trader. The purpose of the opening meeting was to ask the Trader about the tax frauds they had disclosed to HMRC, to ask them about any potential tax frauds they hadn't disclosed and to get the Trader to agree to commission a Disclosure report. The Trader's Tax Advisor would prepare the Disclosure Report, disclosing all of the trader's tax frauds and quantifying how much the trader owed HMRC.

Cassie spoke with a Bristolian accent. Not a comic, "Yeh but no but," nor an over the top, "Av eee" or "Gurt lush", but small differences such as, Cassie did not send out Tax Calculations they were

"Caulkulations." Her accent was genuine and endearing.

When Cassie went to one of these opening meetings she always looked immaculate in one of her very stylish business suits. Some Traders and their Tax Advisors would smile when they saw HMRC had sent a woman, and a blonde at that, and they would smile again when they heard her Bristolian accent. They weren't smiling five or six hours later when she brought the meeting to a close.

Then there was her name, Cassie Holmes-Smith. She had joined Customs and Excise as Cassie Holmes and people knew her as that. As much as she loved Shaun she didn't wish to be one of the countless Smiths on HMRC's General Address list. It always took what seemed like an age to find someone called Smith on the General Address list. More importantly, she was protecting herself and her family from some of the villains she dealt with. Good luck finding Cassie Holmes-Smith online. Cassie had heard all of the Sherlock Holmes jibes over the years, from Traders and their Tax Advisors. A good response which usually shut them up was, "Sherlock Holmes always gets to the truth, well so do I."

Cassie was very bright and could easily have gained promotion to Grade 6 if she had taken what Alan called a "pink and fluffy job." Such as becoming a Champion, of whatever was flavour of the month. Alan had often thought he would like to see one of these Champions who had been promoted ahead of one of his hard-working investigators in a ring with one of them over ten three-minute rounds. Now that would be a promotion selection process worth seeing.

Another job leading to promotion was a job in Policy. A few years ago some bright spark in Policy came up with the acronym UTR for Upstream Tax Revenue. Had these people ever worked a tax enquiry? One of the most common acronyms already used in HMRC was UTR, Unique Tax Reference. If you were an individual or a company self-assessing your tax you would have a Unique Tax Reference.

Policy's latest wheeze was a customer survey at the end of a tax fraud investigation.

"How did we do?" What did they expect the tax fraudsters to reply? "Badly, you didn't find the holiday home in Florida owned via the Cayman Islands' Company, the bank account in Cyprus, not even the £100,000 in cash under the bed."

Cassie had her own ideas for a survey. At the start of a fraud investigation the tax fraudster should be asked:

a) Do you live in a big house?
b) Do you drive a flash car?
c) Do you have a much younger/trophy partner?
d) Do your children go to a private school?

Then, at the end of the investigation, the Trader should be asked questions A,B,C and D again and, if the trader's trophy wife hadn't left him, the children weren't in a bog standard comp and the house and car hadn't been repossessed, then clearly HMRC could do better.

Another Head Office job with a chance of promotion was the "Bean Counter." The Bean Counter's side of a typical conversation between an Investigator and a Bean Counter might go something like this:

"Yes, I understand. You climbed a giant beanstalk, fought with a giant and seized a golden harp, but we need to know how many beans were in the bag you exchanged for the cow."

"We need this data on the case flow system, so we can record the yield from the investigation and how long it has taken. We also need the same data put onto the CPART system, as that allows us to prepare a pretty diagram of the yield from all of the cases for the next Head Office meeting."

"You're fighting another giant as we speak, but can you input the yield data today?"

"What do you mean? There is no yield yet and you have no idea when the investigation will settle. Policy states a Code of Practice 9 case should only take twelve months from start to finish."

"Oh, the giant appealed to the First Tier Tax Tribunal, about our seizing his golden harp. You don't know if his appeal will be successful, therefore you haven't claimed any yield and you don't have a date for the tribunal hearing hence you do not know when the case will close?"

Cassie could have told Policy that she had worked the Code of Practice 9 Investigation from start to finish in less than six months, but that was with the cooperation of the Trader, with a Tax Advisor who didn't take on too many clients and was as keen as Cassie to work the case quickly. All of which was extremely rare.

Alan saw one of his main roles as being to let his Investigators investigate and, as far as humanly possible, let him deal with the Bean Counters.

Nor was dealing with the Bean Counters the worst part of Cassie's job, this could be the Traders themselves. Cassie had dealt with one particularly nasty Trader, who had secretly filmed her at their meeting and then posted images of her online. But how to get images taken down? Senior management, Head Office and the Union, had all been as much use as a chocolate fire guard. Eventually it was Alan who had researched the subject and who had got the images taken down. The Trader had done a runner to Thailand but his campaign against Cassie continued. He had written in total seventeen letters of complaint about Cassie. His every complaint, however ridiculous, had to be dealt with following HMRC's Official Complaint Procedure. He also submitted Subject Access Requests to HMRC for all documents and data connected to Cassie's investigation of him. Cassie spent days going through hundreds of documents checking if each document could be provided and, if not, recording why it couldn't be provided. If it could be provided to him did it need to be redacted? Redaction being a laborious process. And, no sooner than she had finished dealing with his first Subject Access Request within the required 45 day period, he sent her another. All of this time spent dealing with Subject Access Requests and complaints was time wasted when she could have been productive investigating current cases. She felt frustrated by these tax fraudsters who were using HMRC's policies and procedures to delay her and her investigation. It was a ploy that was often used. Nor was it likely that the politicians could help. The woman who had been appointed as the Revenue Adjudicator checking whether HMRC were following the rules was later appointed to check if MPs were following their own expenses rules. She was promptly dismissed by them.

The Trader's complaints came in by letter attached to an email and Cassie would respond to the complaint both by letter to the postal address provided and by email. The Trader had written asking HMRC not to write to him for 3 months, because he was ill and then a month later wrote complaining HMRC hadn't written to him.

A letter had been received from the Trader from a new postal address and when HMRC had posted the reply to the new address, a complaint letter had been received from the trader demanding to know why HMRC had posted a letter to that address.

The trader even complained about the way Cassie signed her letters, but best of all was when the trader made an official complaint that Cassie had made him blind. Only for his sight to miraculously return a few months later.

Cassie wondered if the trader would ever tire of Thailand and the bar girls who featured in almost all the photos he posted online, but she doubted it.

The photos of the bar girls made Cassie remember one of her Dad's Royal Navy stories as one of a group of young sailors receiving instruction from an old Chief Petty Officer. Her Dad recalled the old Chief had said, "Now lads, if you trap a bird in south east Asia, always check the undercarriage." Her Dad and his young mates were all of the same view that the Chief had had a nasty surprise in south east Asia.

Cassie enjoyed being on Alan's team, it was unlike any other. Cassie had noticed that the other teams on their floor didn't tend to socialise together outside the office, often didn't sit together, rarely seemed to collaborate and some didn't even talk to each other. Alan's team was more like a family than a team, people, once they joined the team tended to stay. Alan would find any reason for a team pub social. Team members' birthdays, births of children or grandchildren to people on the team, settling a big case, the list went on. Cassie felt sure that there was no other team in HMRC that regarded the end of the tax year as a reason for a pub social. Failing all of these there was always Poets' Day (Piss Off Early Tomorrow's Saturday) to go to the Seven Stars or on a nice summer's day, the tables outside the Landogger Trow, of Treasure Island fame.

The family wasn't limited to just team members. Retired team members were still part of the family and often were also Alan's golf partners. Cassie had thought that when Alan finally decided he wasn't spending enough time on the golf course and retired she would like Alan's job and the promotion to Grade 6 that came with it.

Another member of the family was a particularly bright young girl called Sally who had left the team for what looked like her dream job, only for it to become a bit of a nightmare. She never left the family though. She sat with the team, was a regular attender at team socials and if you asked anyone in the office not in the know who she worked for they probably would have replied, "She's on Alan's team isn't she?"

Cassie had never seen Alan drunk. Perhaps the closest was the Team's Christmas Do last year.

Getting ready for work that morning the ever-practical Cassie considered carefully what to wear. I'm going to work, we're having our Christmas Party and then I'm picking Wendy up from netball practice. What outfit do I have to cover all three events? I know, smart suit, classy silk blouse and platform trainers, perfect. Finish it off with my gold square link necklace and earrings and a misting of Baccarat Rouge. Some Clarins lip gloss and a Radley clutch. She looked at herself in the mirror and was satisfied with what she saw.

The Christmas do started at 10.30am in The Knights' Templar (the local Wetherspoons). Then began the trilogy starting with The King's Head as it was the first to open its doors. The next stop was The Cornucopia followed by The Shakespeare. "What time is the meal booked for?" Alan asked. "1 pm" came the reply. Alan glanced at his watch, it showed 12.30pm. It was a 15-minute walk to The Shakespeare. "Who's for another?" Alan shouted.

At the restaurant the draught beer selection was reduced to one, Staropramen. They wouldn't be staying here long after the meal, Cassie thought, as she ordered a round from the waiter. "Make mine a Strap on," said Alan. Predictably as soon as the meal was over they were off to the King William Ale

House known as King Billy's, via the Old Fishmarket. While Cassie stayed sober she observed with amusement her colleagues' behaviour become more jovial and relaxed. This wasn't just her team, they were a family and, had she been on a work do with any other group of people, she would have made her excuses and left directly after the meal.

By 8 pm only the hardened few were left, still good company despite their alcohol intake. Cassie, who had been on a selection of soft drinks, because she was picking up Wendy later, looked across at Alan. He had started swaying, not side to side, but back and forth, to angles that would not seem possible.

This brought to mind another of Cassie's colleagues on a works do who, not realising there were three steps between the public bar and the lounge bar of the pub they had been in, had somersaulted through the air and landed on his feet, his glass of whisky still in his hand and cigarette still between his lips. He had then walked on as if nothing had happened.

This cigarette gymnastics had been outdone by her grandfather who would light a cigarette then with his tongue, would flick the lighted cigarette inside his mouth, close his mouth, dive into the sea and then, after reaching the surface, flick the cigarette back out of his mouth so he could smoke as he swam.

Alan had a contented look on his face but he still didn't look drunk. Quite amazing as he had easily had more than two gallons of beer. Alan was smiling while he reminisced about his days working for Special Compliance Office, AKA SCO, AKA the Heavy Mob. An Inland Revenue predecessor of HMRC's Fraud Investigation Service. If you worked for SCO you never wore a suit, the SCO uniform was a long black leather jacket which Alan wore to this day, albeit a few sizes larger than in his SCO days.

Alan was reminiscing about a particular evening when he and three of his leather jacketed colleagues were due to do a Knock. The 5am Knock was on a Cornish fish wholesaler who had not only been under declaring all of his sales, but also had been paying the fishermen half and half, 50% cheque and 50% in cash. So, you can imagine what this meant that the fishermen declared to the tax man. The Knock led to them staying in a pub with rooms, in a little Cornish village. The pub had three rooms and Alan and his colleagues had taken two of them. They had advised the landlord that they would like to pay upfront as they would be away early doors due to being expected early on site.

You could tell that this was the sort of pub where they were used to mopping up the blood and teeth on a Sunday morning, but Alan had just eaten the best fish and chips he'd ever had. Freshly caught fish, battered by the landlady, with home-made tartare sauce and fresh peas. Some swanky London restaurant could easily have charged ten times what Alan had paid for the meal and still not be overcharging.

A little later two young men had walked in, dressed in dark suits and ties with shiny square ID badges on their lapels.. They had taken the last room and had asked about food, only to be advised that the kitchen had closed, but the landlord could make them some sandwiches. Accepting this offer, they inquired about the non-alcoholic drinks menu. Having declined Pepsi they settled on two glasses of lemonade.

The two young men had just left to go to their room when Alan went to the bar. It was the sixth and last round of the evening, they had an early start after all. They each had been sampling the wide selection of real ales available, Alan was particularly keen on a local IPA. As he got to the bar one of the tough looking locals said to the landlord glancing in the direction that the two young men had departed, "Bloody Revenue is in." Alan didn't know who the two young men were, Mormon missionaries perhaps, but they certainly weren't Revenue. The incident had amused Alan at the time and still did, hence the smile on his face as he rocked back and forth.

Alan's team worked in a shiny new Bristol regional centre. It may have been new but it didn't feel like home. Most likely because no-one had their own desk. Every desk was a hot desk. So, at the end of the day, you couldn't leave out photos of loved ones or your Bristol City or Bristol Rovers mug, depending on whether you supported the Gas or the Robins. This was because it wasn't your desk. Woe betide anyone returning refreshed from their holiday who placed their holiday biscuits on one of the small and extremely rare storage units as this would be seen by the hot desk police as the equivalent of a predatory land grab. The way around hot desking was to get in early and grab your desk. No-one seemed to dare to hot desk and sit at one of the desks on Alan's team. Cassie, therefore, did have a desk she sat at every day just don't tell the Hot Desk Police. It still didn't feel like home though, like the last two offices the team had worked in. Cassie recalled when they had moved into the office before last. Two, now retired, colleagues had the following conversation:

"Look there, you can see my house from here."

"Which one is it?"

"It's the one next door to the house that used to have blue blinds."

Or two colleagues discussing the theatre:
"Of course, Olivier played Hamlet."

Alan: "Really, who won?"

In the old office Cassie had photos on her desk of her and Shaun and Wendy and Barney and their dog Boo, whilst Alan would only have a coffee cup on his desk on which was written, "Guilty until proven Innocent." Alan would take his mug home, once a year, for a clean whether it needed it or not.

Behind Alan's desk had been a notice board to which were attached photos cut from newspapers, some with handwritten speech bubbles coming out of their mouths. To the uninitiated this was all meaningless but the team knew what it was. A trophy wall with the scalps the team had taken.

One of the photos cut from a daily newspaper's tv guide was for Antiques Road Trip. Cassie had investigated an antiques dealer who had been selling antique mirrors to the Americans by the shipping container load, without declaring any of the profits to HMRC. He had built up a property portfolio in Bristol of over 80 properties, but they had been financed by refinancing the existing properties. After a 3-year investigation with a complete lack of cooperation from the antiques dealer, Cassie had issued Assessments of Tax and Penalties which, at first, the antiques dealer had appealed and threatened to take to the Tax Tribunal. He had, however, then declared himself bankrupt, his properties being repossessed. A few months after he had been made bankrupt he had asked for a meeting with Cassie. Cassie didn't know why he had asked for a meeting and wasn't much more the wiser after she had met with the antiques dealer, apart from him saying he would pay back all he owed. He seemed to want to make it known to HMRC that he was done with the antiques game. The statement that he would pay back all that he owed was almost certainly a lie.

Being told lies was part of the job. Cassie had learned the sure fire way of knowing that a Trader was lying was, if the Trader began by saying, "On my kids' lives I'm telling the truth."

A couple of years after her meeting with the bankrupt antiques dealer Cassie had one of those very few moments when she had 5-10 minutes with nothing particular to do. She turned on the tv and was flicking aimlessly through the channels, when all of a sudden Antiques Road Trip made her pause. If you have seen the programme once you know the format:

"I like that," says the celebrity.

"Let's ask the dealer for his best price," says the quirky antiques expert.

Forward steps the antiques dealer. It was the antiques dealer she had investigated who had told her he was done with the antiques game. Cassie watched the programme through to the end. It had clearly been filmed last summer and any trading should have been mentioned on the antiques dealer's last tax return. The next day Cassie checked the antiques dealer's tax return and he had failed to declare income from his antiques trade.

Cassie mentioned this to Alan. "Arthur Negus at it again," said Alan, thoughts of a mechanical singing bird in his head as Cassie looked at him blankly. "Report it to Criminal but they probably won't want it, just one year you say?" Alan queried. Cassie nodded, "He's a tiddler, throw him back, give it five years, then reel him in," Alan advised.

The Antiques Road Trip newspaper cutting had gone up on the board. Not just a past scalp, but a potential future one as well.

Alan had seen Antiques Road Trip and he had his own idea on what the antique dealers should say:

An actress famous in the 1970's: "You have labelled this at £50, what's your best price?"

Alan: "£50".

Actress famous in the 1970s: "What if I give you a kiss?"

Alan: "£49.99".

Actress famous in the 1970's: "Is there absolutely nothing you can do about the price?"

Alan: "Yes, pass it here."

The actress duly passes the antique to Alan, who crosses out £50, writes on £60 and passes it back to her.

CHAPTER THREE

Alan wandered over to Cassie's desk and said, "I've just emailed you a new case to review based on Intel received. Mossi Moscovitch, AKA David Levin, AKA Joseph Blum, AKA David Kaufman, AKA Joseph Kahan, AKA Robert Barratt."

Cassie repeated the name Robert Barratt which didn't match the other aliases.

"Probably a scam linked to helicopter finance," Alan said with a twinkle in his eye. Alan's joke flew over Cassie's head like a white helicopter in the 1980's Barratt's Homes adverts he was joking about. Although Alan was still smiling at his Barratt's Homes reference, he was often the only person who understood and laughed at his jokes, his mind had moved on to a common theme of thought, the good old days. In the good old days when you gave an investigator a case to review it would be a big chunky file which you could thump on their desk. Oh how he missed those days.

Cassie, having read the Intel, decided to have a search done for any other Intel reports linked to Mossi Moscovitch. She would also search HMRC's systems for any connection to any land and property transactions using Mossi's name and the aliases. This could take days or often weeks of searching but once she had those results she would decide where to go from there.

Alan hadn't been too far out when he joked that Mossi had used the name Robert Barratt in a helicopter finance scam. The scam had in fact involved airport car parking spaces. Mossi had set up the website selling car parking spaces and advertised in China, south east Asia and the Middle east. The websites have a generic picture of a smiling businessman labelled, "our CEO Robert Barratt".

The advert stated that this was, "High return investment, for High Networth Individuals." Much further down in the small print it was mentioned that this was an unregulated investment. There were graphs and charts showing the expansion of airports in the UK and expected revenues for each car parking space. The price of the car parking space was a very reasonable $22,000 US or $40,000 US for two. The website warned that these prices would not stay this low for long so now is the time to invest. Investors should send their cheques to Airport Parking UK, PO Box 139, London, NW17 1BJ. In return investors would receive a land registry document indicating the location of the car park, an architect's drawing of what the car park would look like and a certificate for the individual car parking space the investor had purchased, signed by Robert Barratt personally. Of course, the investors weren't High Networth Individuals but greedy people who couldn't resist an offer too good to be true and, of course, if it all looks too good to be true, it generally is.

Mossi had rented for six months, with an option to buy, a piece of farmland on which previously five cars could be parked and charged for airport parking as the farm was near the East Midlands Airport. Only these five spaces were tarmacked. The remainder was grass and mud. The farmer had been contacted by phone and email, he had never met Robert Barratt and the payment the farmer had received was transferred via a money service bureau that ceased trading two weeks later. A common occurrence in the money laundering process.

This was the car park in which 250 car parking spaces, costing $22,000 US each were being sold. The cheques were soon rolling in. Mossi was a major figure in the money laundering business of his community's underworld so turning cheques written to Airport Parking UK into untraceable money was a run of the mill task for him. Mossi had sublet the land as valet airport parking to a traveller family he had done business with before. They had paid him in, shall we call it, "second hand" jewellery. Mossi had the contacts to move this on.

Alan had his own terminology for the travellers. It might not meet HMRC's latest guidance but it was accurate and, being Alan, it had a 1970's TV show connection, 'The Gone Tomorrow People.'
For ten weeks the Airport Valet Parking cash-only business had worked quite well. Cash only, no card but they would take Euros, Dollars, etc, at their own rate of exchange, of course. The Gone Tomorrow People were already in profit over what they could have got for the second-hand jewellery. There were obviously complaints when the cars were returned to their owners caked in mud but, one look at the Gone Tomorrow People and the complainants decided, "We will just not park there again".

Then, one afternoon, some of the younger Gone Tomorrow People decided to have a race to see which of the parked cars was the fastest. After three of the cars had been written off they told their parents. Within the hour the Gone Tomorrow People were gone today. Dumping a wooden box containing a jumble of car keys on the farmer's doorstep. For the next few weeks the farmer had to deal with angry car owners turning up by taxi. Three of the car owners were a lot more angry than most.

Despite all the hassle the farmer had received six months' rent for ten weeks' use and having lost his subsidies from the EU because of Brexit he was grateful for any new income stream. The Gone Tomorrow People had made a profit. Mossi, though, had made ten times more from the investors than what it had cost him in advertising and setting up the website.

He had even made a small profit from the sale of the second-hand jewellery, less what he had paid the farmer. Or, to be precise, a company called Hair Today Ltd had made a payment via the no longer existent money service bureau. Hair Today Ltd was subsequently struck from Companies House for not having submitted accounts. Hair Today Ltd had received the payment via the Money Service Bureau from a building firm in Poland and there were multiple further layers of money laundering between the Polish building firm and the account Mossi had actually used to make the payment. The investors meanwhile had paid $22,000 for a piece of paper signed by the non-existent Robert Barratt.

Cassie had her own experience of airport parking. She lived near Bristol Airport and, being chairwoman of the local Residents Association, she was well aware how fed up the local people were with cars being parked on their streets by people trying to avoid paying airport parking fees while on holiday and then a few weeks ago it happened to her.

Wendy had been appointed as director of the school fashion show. She had every second of the show planned. No-one would put a foot on the catwalk without a signal from her. On the night of the fashion show Wendy had her hair, makeup and outfit, just right. She called down to her mum to say she was ready. As Cassie and Wendy left the house Cassie's face dropped, someone had parked on their drive blocking her in. "Bloody cheek," thought Cassie, "whose car is that?" Then she realised it had happened to her, her drive was being used for airport parking. Cassie rang Shaun who was still at work. He ran a mobile tyre fitting business. Shaun was just finishing a job and he said he would be home as soon as he could. Shaun got back in twenty minutes and seconds later, was driving Cassie and a very disgruntled Wendy to the school.

In typical heroic Mum-style despite the outrageous car parking incident on her drive she had still managed to get Wendy to the Fashion Show on time. As they arrived Wendy jumped out of the van slamming the door violently behind her as she ran into the school while Cassie, biting her tongue, breathing slowly and deeply to keep herself calm, leaned across to Shaun, kissed him on the cheek, squeezed his arm and looked into his eyes. He knew better than to say anything at that point, the look that she gave him said it all.

The show was a success, Cassie had sat in the front row watching with pride as the show came to an end. Wendy could be completely focused, committed and ruthless when it came to completing a challenge. Often not realising the sacrifices her parents made in order for her to do this and this show was no exception. She and Shaun had spent hours of being Mum and Dad's taxi service in the evenings leading up to the show waiting in their car in the school car park evening after evening when they would rather have been at home having a glass of wine and relaxing in a hot bath after a hard day's work. But Cassie didn't mind because she recognised that Wendy was her Mini-Me, Cassie had been exactly the same at that age but she didn't dare voice that thought to Wendy because she knew the reaction she would get from her daughter if she did. It wasn't worth the pain.

The next day Cassie rang Alan to explain that she would be taking a day off. By lunchtime Shaun and some mates had manoeuvred Cassie's car into a position where it could be driven off the drive. The offending vehicle was up on bricks, with neat piles of four wheels and four tyres alongside it. Consequently, Cassie had gaffer taped two envelopes and a note with her telephone number on it to the car windscreen. Two weeks after the night of the school fashion show the phone call came that Cassie had been looking forward to.

The woman said, "What have you done to my car?"

Cassie replied, "Do you mean the vehicle abandoned on my land?"

The woman did not respond. Cassie suggested the woman might want to open the envelopes. The woman did so and then exclaimed, "What's this?"

Cassie explained that the white envelope contained a copy of an email she had sent to the police advising that a vehicle had been dumped on her land and that she had checked DVLA's website and the vehicle's MOT had expired last week. She, therefore, understood that it would be illegal for the vehicle to be driven until it had a current MOT certificate. The brown envelope contained notice that the abandoned vehicle would be sold, if not removed within seven days, and the seven days had expired five days ago.

The woman shrieked, "But I have two small children."

"Not my problem," Cassie replied.

"We have luggage," the woman cried.

"Not my problem," Cassie replied again.

"I will go to the police," the woman tried half-heartedly.

"Good luck with that. The car will be going to British Car Auctions at 3pm today," Cassie explained. The woman fell silent.

"Would you like me to help you?" Cassie asked. The woman replied that she did.
Cassie explained that for £500 plus VAT the woman's car could be towed to a local MOT garage, with four wheels, complete with tyres, back on.

"That's daylight robbery, there must be a local garage that can do it cheaper." The woman had returned to shrieking.

"The local garage owners are as fed up as all the other residents with inconsiderate tightwads like yourself parking on our streets. Or, in your case, abandoning your soon to be auctioned vehicle on my land," Cassie replied.

"This is so unfair," the woman screamed. Cassie was unphased, she heard this complaint all the time, usually from the taxpayers she was investigating.

Cassie looked out the window. It had started to rain. She hoped that it was raining at home and she wasn't disappointed. The woman's next comment was, "Oh my God, it's raining now."

"Oh dear," Cassie replied, unable to keep the mirth from her voice. The woman first screamed in anger and then cried, or perhaps it was one of the children crying, it was hard to tell because of the beating of the rain.

"Do you want me to help you or not?" Cassie asked.

Cassie took the mumbled response for a yes and rang Shaun to let him know he had a £500 job, but she said, "Make sure she pays upfront before you lift a finger."

As Cassie put her mobile phone back in her handbag she caught Alan smiling at her.

"Not a happy bunny," he commented.

"No," Cassie replied.

"Oh what a pity, never mind," said Alan.

A few hours later Cassie rang Shaun for an update. "Which MOT garage did you take her to?" Cassi asked. Shaun replied he had taken the offending car to Bill Collett's garage. Unfortunately, she would be away later this afternoon. The list of required work was all quick to do, new wiper blades, two new tyres, new exhaust, brake pads, rear fog lamp bulb and rear number plate bulb.

Disgruntedly Shaun said, "She should be back in the Cotswolds this afternoon. You should have seen the size of the rock on her finger. You know the type – "What's your village?" Cassie did know the type and thought, "Well yes, that's what happens when you mess with me."

CHAPTER FOUR

A few months ago, Cassie had listened to the BBC podcast, "The Unorthodox Life of Miriam." The podcast gave one woman's description of the Orthodox Jewish Community in which Mossi operated. She explained how it's commonplace, within the community to which she belonged, to purchase property in a name other than your own. Using false documentation, so as to facilitate claiming housing benefit on a house you actually own. She explained that advisors within her community would assist people like her and her husband to obtain documentary evidence of jobs they didn't have showing payments for sixteen hours a week, so as to maximise the benefits that could be claimed. When in actual fact a person would be working full time "on the black," for cash in hand, or cheques exchangeable for cash.

Then there was the newspaper article Cassie had read about the prosecution of Edward Cohen, also from the community in which Mossi operated. Cohen had laundered over ten million pounds through the bank accounts for various charities within the community which he had earned from the sale of fake Viagra. In addition, he had been prosecuted for claiming housing benefit on a property he actually owned.

Mossi's parents were not rich or powerful, but little people like Miriam and her husband. He despised them and had nothing to do with them.

Like all teenage boys in the community Mossi had attended a Yeshiva to further his religious education. It was here that he gained his reputation as a bully and for violence. When one of the teachers made a mistake of hitting the fifteen-year-old Mossi, Mossi had beaten the teacher so badly that he never returned to work and even now walked with a stick. There was no police involvement, like everything else in the community it was dealt with within the community and, whilst many had been horrified, one of the rich families, the Solomons, had seen promise and two years later Mossi was working for them, collecting rents for them from the illegal immigrants they housed. These were illegal immigrants who had paid off their traffickers and who now relied on the black economy, prostitution or crime to pay their rent. Most struggled to pay the rent charged for the tiny rooms in the badly maintained buildings owned by the Solomons. Mossi had no qualms about violence man, woman or child he would beat them up. He wasn't sadistic, he got no pleasure from violence, it was just his job and he was good at it. His favourite trick, if there were children present, was to take a child by the arm or the leg and hold the child out a window, or over a bannister, anywhere with a big drop, until the parents or parent came up with the rent. Most of the time though, the tenants were single young men and he found the most effective method with them was to beat them until they were prostrate on the floor and then produce his Bowie knife and ask them if they want to pay the rent or lose their bollocks.

Mossi liked girls but he didn't want to do what the little people did, marry young and have enough kids for a football team, so he used prostitutes, often in return for a few days' grace with payment of the rent. There was a rumour that when Mossi was eighteen one of the illegal immigrants had fought back. Mossi had throttled him to death. The body had been stripped and dumped in the Thames.

By the age of 21 Mossi was acting as bodyguard to Mordecai Solomon, an international money launderer, travelling to Belgium, Switzerland, Israel and New York.

Now aged 28, Mossi was the Solomons' contact point with the organised crime groups, for whom money was laundered. Mossi and others like him provided a buffer between the Solomons and the crime.

This week it was an organised crime group (OCG) from Dublin. They had a factory in Bulgaria which produced near perfect fake cigarettes of the main UK brands. The organised crime group sold the cigarettes north and south of the border and were bringing them into Ireland by the lorry load. Therefore, the OCG had a lot of cash they wanted converting into property. When Patrick, the OCG's representative, had met Mossi for the first time, Mossi had told him that converting cash into property would be no problem and it hadn't been. The cash had been converted into flats in Dubai and the boss back in Dublin was pleased. Patrick had been impressed when he first entered the communities' area of London, it was like travelling to another country. Patrick had done business in Republican Belfast and, there like here, he got the feeling a sparrow couldn't fart without it being known about.

On their first meeting Mossi had led him into a nondescript house, into its basement, through what must have been the cellars of at least three houses and then through two massive doors that wouldn't have disgraced Fort Knox, to enter into what could best be described as a bank. Which was just a tiny part of the network by which the OCG's cash would be converted into property.

Everyone in the community knew Mossi and everyone knew you didn't mess with Mossi.

CHAPTER FIVE

Cassie had completed a review of Mossi and was discussing the results with Alan. She looked out of the window, "I can see why Alan prefers to sit at this desk." The view from the window allowed him to watch the trains coming and going at Bristol Temple Meads station and he had a view of the river where he could watch the taxi boats ferrying commuters from the station around the city to their various destinations. It certainly beat taking the bus. Compared to other workstations in the office whose only view of the outside world was a mural of Clifton Suspension Bridge, designed and built by the same engineer as Bristol Temple Meads Station. The engineer in question, Isambard Kingdom Brunel was also responsible for another historic attraction in the city which lived on the river, the SS Great Britain. Conveniently the river taxis could take you there as well. So, Alan's desk was well placed. She was amazed that she remembered these facts about Bristol, she couldn't even remember when she had learned about them. It must be something that's drummed into you at school from an early age if you were local.

After hours of research Cassie had found no assets in Mossi's name. No property, freehold or leasehold, stranger still there were no liabilities, no mortgage, no car finance, not even a contract mobile phone. There were some comments online about Robert Barratt being a con artist, but even if she could follow the money could she tax it? Was there ever a trade, or just a con?

In HMRC there was the principle of tainted by illegality, for example the profits from the sale of illegal drugs were taxable. The sale of drugs was taxable, after all Boots the Chemist sold drugs and paid tax on the profits. In contrast the proceeds of kidnap were not taxable. Not that there was a lot of kidnapping in Bristol, although Shaun might disagree when Cassie dragged him to IKEA.

Robert Barratt aside, Mossi's other false names were so common that finding a property in any of these names which related to Mossi would likely be like searching for a needle in a haystack. Despite this Cassie tried her luck but none were found. She had absentmindedly managed to eat a whole pot of hummus and too many breadsticks to sustain her through her searches so focused was she on her task that she wasn't keeping track of what she was eating. As far as she could tell Mossi had not purchased property in any of these false names. "Damn," she thought, "I could have saved the hummus calories and used them on a glass of wine this evening." Mossi appeared never to have been an officer of a company. He had not claimed benefits. He had no Unique Tax reference tax record. Nor was there any record of him ever having had any form of employment reported to HMRC. A check of the Home Office systems revealed he had been born in the UK and there was no indication that he had lived abroad. Although Intel showed Mossi was a regular international traveller, Switzerland, the USA, the Middle East, Eastern Europe, Belgium, The Netherlands, Israel and what appeared to be holiday destinations Costa Rica, The Gambia and Thailand. Mossi was, in short, a ghost, albeit an international, jet-setting ghost.

Cassie thought to herself about how hard it had been for her and Shaun to save the money to take the family to Greece last summer even though they both worked full time and lived quite modest lives, so how was Mossi paying for all of this international travel? She was used to hearing explanations that the traders she investigated lived on fresh air and had even investigated a man with assets but no income who turned out to be a national lottery winner. Mossi, however, seemed more likely to be living on the proceeds of crime.

The Intel did, however, link Mossi to three UK companies although Companies House' records showed no connection between Mossi and any of these companies. Cassie's suggested way forward was that she looked at these three companies. Alan liked his Investigators to follow their nose and Cassie was certainly doing that. Cassie explained to Alan that there wasn't enough for a Code of Practice 9 Investigation, but she wanted to look at these three companies and see where it took her.

Alan leaned back in his chair, clasped his hands behind his head and, looking like a 1970s cop discussing a case with a colleague (the only thing that was missing from this scene was a lit cigarette), crossed his legs with his ankle resting on his knee. He suggested as he often did, "Poke it with a stick and see what you find. That's what we would have done in the good old days." "You never left them," Cassie thought, smiling to herself.

Of course, the good old days are relative. When Alan had begun to work for the Inland Revenue all those years ago, the old blokes in the office (who, thinking back were probably a lot younger than Alan was now), had told him about the good old days. After the second world war alcoholic spirits were still rationed but two of the Tax Inspectors in the office had been Prisoners of War. Rather than escaping they had put their efforts into learning how to build and operate a Still. The two former POWs had built a Still in the cellar of the Inland Revenue

Tax Office. The office Christmas parties certainly went with a swing, just don't tell Customs and Excise.

The first company that Cassie looked at was Wheat Ear Ltd. The company had not submitted accounts to Companies House and Companies House was about to dissolve the company for not having done so. A Land Registry check revealed that Wheat Ear Ltd had been connected to a piece of land. Presumably farming land, but this had been sold to Redland Farm Ltd for £2,000,000. So all Cassie knew was that Wheat Ear Ltd had somehow acquired some land and sold it for £2,000,000. Cassie could find no record of Wheat Ear Ltd registering the purchase of the land it had sold so she didn't know if this land was sold at a profit or a loss. There was no charge registered at Companies House against the land. So how did Wheat Ear Ltd fund the purchase of the land it had sold?

Cassie notified Companies House that HMRC had an objection to the striking off of Wheat Ear Ltd. She asked the Valuation Office Agency (VOA) for a not negotiated valuation of the land sold by Wheat Eat Ltd to Redland Farms Ltd. In other words, what did the VOA think that the land was worth?

The Director and Sole Shareholder of Wheat Ear Ltd per Companies House had an address in Israel and an occupation of student. "Just another patsy," thought Cassie. "A perfect example of how criminals use unpoliced systems to work in their favour."

The Director of the other company, Redland Farms Ltd, looked more interesting, Sandra Williams. Cassie checked the address given for Sandra Williams, it was the offices of a Tax Advisor, so not much help unless she was a client of his and Cassie could check Sandra Williams' tax record that way. Even then Cassie would need access to systems she didn't have, to trace the Agent and get a list of the clients for whom she had submitted tax returns. Cassie decided instead to check HMRC systems for every S Williams with the month and year of birth that Sandra Williams had recorded on Companies House's records. A quick task if you were searching for Gilbert Peregrine, an old boss of Cassie's, not so quick when you have to check every S Williams. Sod's Law was if you were searching for someone with a date of birth in January 1973, the date of birth would be 31st January 1973, but on this occasion Cassie was lucky. She had only got to the 5th of the month when she located Sandra Williams. There was a Unique Tax Reference and Tax Returns for the past six years. On her last two Tax Returns she declared her taxable income as £12,000 UK Dividends. She had also on her last two tax returns completed an Employment Income page and, whilst not declaring any employment income, Sandra Williams had declared that the employer's name was Redland Farms Ltd. So, Cassie had found the S Williams she was looking for. The tax returns submitted by Sandra Williams for earlier years had declared self-employment income, with a trade of entertainment.

Sandra Williams, known to everyone as Sandy, was a former prostitute and Mossi had been one of her regulars. Sandy had grown up in the upstairs flat of a council maisonette in the Clase area of Swansea. An only child to a single mum. Her mum had furnished the council flat as best she could, second hand carpets and off cuts, which often didn't reach the walls. But these gaps were covered by furniture bought in Morriston, from John the Con's second-hand shop or covered by mats. Sandy's mum supplemented her benefits by working cash in hand a couple of nights a week as a barmaid at the local pub, The Wildfowler. This extra cash she spent on her Saturday nights out, usually at The Wildfowler. If she was feeling really flush she would go to the Top Rank in Swansea instead. A Saturday night in The Wildfowler could best be described by the pub's local nickname, "The Chuck-a-Chair." As a little girl Sandy had liked Saturday nights, as she would be looked after by Aunty Mair, who would give her chocolate biscuits, something not to be found at home. Mair was no relation, just an older lady who lived in the downstairs flat of the maisonette.

Sandy grew up to become a very pretty petite blonde. By the age of seventeen she was working as a barmaid in The Wildfowler, albeit under age and, of course, cash in hand. After she had been working there for three months a man came in one night who told her he was a model scout and he could guarantee her work if she moved up to London. She took his number and within days stood at Paddington Station, suitcase in hand and her head full of dreams of being a supermodel and travelling the world.

The man was true to his word and she did get modelling work, for soft porn magazines with titles like "Jail Bait" and "Barely Legal." The closest she got to travelling the world was a photoshoot in Hounslow for a Japanese magazine, only to be told that at seventeen she looked too old for the Japanese market. After about eighteen months the "Jail Bait" and "Barely Legal" work dried up. She couldn't find any other soft porn work. The hard porn work she was offered wasn't well paid and not that regular. Bar work helped but it didn't pay the high rents in London and this was how Sandy became a prostitute.

Quite a few years later she met Mossi. After he had been paying her for just over a year, one night he had made her an offer. He would provide her with a little cottage down in Kent, all bills paid and a regular income. All she had to do was pretend she owned the land that he actually owned. She didn't need to farm it as all the land was rented as tack to local farmers. Of course, if he should be in the area and stay the night, he wouldn't expect to pay. Sandy asked if she could have a dog, Mossi nodded. Then she asked if she could keep a donkey and when Mossi once again agreed, she accepted his proposal and sealed it with a kiss.

Whilst working as a bodyguard for the international money launderer Mordecai Solomon, Mossi had been approached with a business opportunity by a young entrepreneur from the community in New York called Chaim Yedlin. Chaim Yedlin arranged to meet Mossi in a bar called Finnegan's, in the area of Manhattan principally populated by Koreans. Mossi assumed Chaim had arranged their meeting outside the community's area of New York to keep it secret.

The bar wouldn't have looked out of place on the TV show 'Cheers'. It had large mirrors behind the bar, and high bar stools along its length, with a brass rail at the bottom where you could rest your feet. There was even a South Korean version of Norm sitting at one end on his own. Mossi arrived fifteen minutes early and Chaim was half an hour late. So Mossi killed time chatting to the barman, Michael from Cork, whom he discovered was working in the USA illegally. From Michael he learned how this business worked. There were three floors to the building, the first floor was where the bar was located, the second floor was a restaurant, but the real money was made on the third floor where Korean business men met with escort girls. After a while Michael's mate John came in for a beer. No money changed hands, obviously their arrangement. John was from County Sligo, also working illegally as a barman but in Queens. He interestingly mentioned that one of his regulars was a Colombian hit man who was living in New York on a retainer, until he got a phone call advising him that his services were required. Mossi, Michael and John were discussing football when Chaim Yedlin arrived. Specifically, if Liverpool was meant to be a Catholic football team and Everton the Protestant football team, how come Everton had been previously called Saint Domingo's Catholic school team?

Chaim was in his early thirties, 6'2", wearing a dark suit and dark tie in an attempt to create the illusion of slimming down his large silhouette. His flabby neck bulged over the collar of the white shirt he was wearing, his hair was in the traditional Ultra-Orthodox Jewish style with Payos, or side curls, dripping wet from the rain outside. Despite his height and bulk he looked vulnerable beside Mossi. Mossi was 5'10" and his shirt bulged not with fat over the collar, but with muscle underneath and his head partly bald and a Number 1 haircut. Menace oozed from every pore.

Chaim ordered the drinks and carried his and Mossi's drinks to a quiet table, then set out his plan for Mossi.

"I have some land in Florida which I intend to sell off plan for condominiums. I have set up a company to sell the land in which I have been selling tokens. I encourage customers to buy tokens which give them a share of the profits that would arise from the sale of the condos by the company, but they would get extra tokens by selling more tokens to new investors. The more tokens they sell the bigger the share of the profits they get."

"The land is worthless I assume?" Mossi enquired. Chaim nodded.

"So, you're operating a Ponzi scheme?" Mossi stated. Chaim nodded again.

"Where do I come in?" Mossi asked.

Chaim explained, "I need to know who in our Community in London is greedy enough to invest but won't break my legs when they lose their money."

"I can do that, what are you offering?" Mossi asked.

"Five per cent of the UK investment received" Chaim replied. Mossi raised his glass and chinked it against Chaim's as he announced, "Deal."

The scheme turned out to be a huge success. Due to a very good sales pitch by Chaim and his sales team, but mainly due to the trust in the Community, both sides of the pond, that one of their own Community would not be so dishonest with them. Then greed had led to a frenzy of purchasing and selling tokens in the worthless swampland. UK sales alone were £120 million giving Mossi a commission of £6 million.

That had been some years ago. The FBI had eventually caught up with Chaim Yedlin and he was currently awaiting trial. Chaim's lawyer was confident that even if he was found guilty, he could appeal and failing that there was always a chance of a Presidential pardon, which Chaim's lawyer had managed to obtain for another client, albeit under President Trump. Mossi, however, had earned £6 million and no-one besides Chaim was aware of his involvement. The £6 million had been laundered through multiple layers and in the case where hundreds of millions of dollars had gone to the main suspect, £6 million was not worth the Government's time to pursue.

A year or so after Mossi received the £6 million a career criminal, Dave "Stripey" Badger, had approached the Solomons, through a contact, for a loan. The purpose of the loan was to fund the importation into the UK of hand rolling tobacco, by the lorry load. By not paying tax and duty on the tobacco Stripey aimed to make millions of pounds a month, but he needed start-up capital, hence the request for a loan from the Solomons. The loan agreed from the Solomons to Stripey was £5 million repayable in one year with £1,250,000 interest. Stripey had insisted that his usual Kent based money launderer handle the money transferred, etc.

To the outside world Simon Chapman was a philanthropist. A leading light in the equestrian world, but to organised crime in the south east of England and beyond, he was known as a money launderer you could trust. The leaders of organised crime groups would not only use him to launder the proceeds of crime, but also to pay each other for services rendered and even on occasion his bank account had been used to pay personal bets between rival OCG leaders.

Unfortunately for Stripey his smuggling operation had been busted by an undercover sting operation by HMRC and the National Crime Agency. Stripey had managed to get away but was convicted in his absence and sentenced to 20 years. As unpleasant as 20 years of Porridge sounded, it wasn't as unpleasant as the consequence of not paying the Solomons back their money. If, of course, they could find him.

The Solomons wanted financial compensation. Their only point of contact was Simon Chapman and so Mossi was sent by the Solomons to negotiate with him.

Mossi drove the Lexus he had borrowed from the Solomons up the drive. The drive appeared to go on forever, either side of the drive were fields in which horses were grazing and, even to Mossi's untrained eye, it was clear that these horses were each valuable assets and not some old nags. The drive eventually ended and Mossi drove onto a vast area of expensive flagstone in the shape of a semicircle at the base of which was a large modern house, with stables either side of it. In front of the house were three cars, an Aston Martin Vanquish, a Jensen Interceptor and a Rolls Royce Silver Ghost. A girl came from a doorway in the house. She was about Mossi's age, pretty, fresh faced with blonde hair and a riding cap she was wearing. The horsey attire was completed by jodhpurs and a black riding jacket. Mossi got out of the Lexus and as he took his first step towards the girl he noticed a man had come into view from one of the stables. The man was dressed in a tweed suit, checked shirt and tie, with a shotgun broken over his arm. Whilst the girl smiled as she approached Mossi, the man's face was immobile and his gaze never left Mossi.

"Mr Chapman's expecting you," the girl said, "I'll show you the way." A few minutes later Mossi was shown into what the girl referred to as "Mr Chapman's study." A man, who Mossi took to be Simon Chapman, was sitting behind perhaps the largest desk Mossi had ever seen. The room was very country house in decoration with paintings of horses and hunting scenes, including one painting behind Chapman's head of a horse with a groom. Simon Chapman was about 6'2", in his early fifties, with a ruddy face, salt and pepper hair and a barrel-like chest.

"Do come in," said Chapman before adding, "what should I call you?"

As he was representing the Solomon family Mossi thought that this was no time for pseudonyms and so replied, "You can call me Mossi."

"You can call me Mr Chapman, do take a seat," Chapman said waving towards one of the two chairs located opposite his. Mossi took a seat, the painting of the horse catching his attention as he did so. He realised once he had sat down that Chapman had produced a revolver and it was now sitting on the desk pointing in his direction, less than an inch from Chapman's right hand.

"It's a Stubbs," said Chapman.

"I thought it was a Smith and Wesson," thought Mossi oblivious to what Chapman had been referring to. Chapman took Mossi's silence to be due to ignorance of the Stubbs painting which rather annoyed him, because he usually enjoyed telling people how much it was worth. So, instead, he began the business conversation.

"I am under no contractual obligation to make any payments on behalf of the unfortunate Mr Badger, but I have a reputation to retain and so I will make your employers an offer of recompense. I have some farmland that I will give them, it's worth the thick edge of £5 million. Jenny will give you the paperwork on your way out. It's a take it or leave it offer."

Mossi's eyes had not left the revolver and the revolver was still pointed at his heart. He knew that he was beaten.

"Good day," said Chapman, wafting Mossi away with the revolver, like smoke from a cigar.

The Solomons weren't happy with the offer, what did they want with farmland in Kent? Mossi saw an opportunity to hide some of his Ponzi scheme commission and offered £4,250,000 for the land. The Solomons decided that £4,250,000 paid now, on a £5 million loan to someone on the run, was a good result.

The land was owned by the St John Smith-Pipkin trust and, by a Letter of Wishes to the Trustees from the beneficiary which was seen only by the Trust's solicitors, the land was transferred to Wheat Ear Ltd.

Cassie scanned her emails. Some could be deleted on sight, others she marked to read later. What she was looking for was anything to progress her investigations. Oh, a response from the VOA on the land sold by Wheat Ear Ltd for £2 million. Three weeks, that was quick, albeit for their own valuation of the land. Opening the attached Valuation Document Cassie scrolled down through to get to the all- important valuation figure, which was £5 million. Why sell land for £2 million which was worth £5 million?

Cassie raised Corporation Tax Determinations on Wheat Ear Ltd in respect of the two corporation tax years for which the company had not submitted corporation tax returns. The intention of Cassie raising the determinations was that the tax determined would be due and payable by the company. This had two advantages; Firstly, this created a tax debt which could be pursued by HMRC and used to liquidate the company, secondly the company could not appeal against the determinations. The company could only replace the determinations by submitting the outstanding Corporation Tax returns. Once these were submitted, HMRC could then open enquiries into the

Corporation Tax Returns to check if they were correct.

CHAPTER SIX

The second of the companies connected by Intel to Mossi was a food wholesaler, based in Pontypridd in Wales, Celtic Foods Limited. The company had been on its last legs for a while and, despite having a large warehouse which it rented, a workforce of 280 and a reasonable reputation in the business, margins were tight and, put simply, they were being pushed out by the big boys.

The warehouse was nestled in the valley on an industrial estate which had been built in the 1970s. The two adjoining businesses were now empty and, aside from a meat pie factory, the industrial estate was empty. The empty units appeared to be a Mecca for Pontypridd's Wanna be Banksies. Not that anyone would pay anything for the graffiti that covered these buildings. The only other sign of thriving life were the sheep nibbling at the weeds growing through the concreted parking spaces outside the unused buildings.

Mossi had contacted the company, by phone and email, explaining that he was Chief of Staff to an Ultra High Net Worth individual who wished to remain anonymous. Mossi offered the shareholders of the company £500,000, £50,000 of which would be paid upfront as a gesture of goodwill. Mossi explained to the shareholders that this was a very small investment for the Ultra High Net Worth individual and that therefore it might take six months for him to find the time to sit down and sign the papers.

Mossi explained that all the senior management would have to go because a new dynamic team would be appointed, this was because the Ultra High Net Worth individual would want instant results. Mossi, as his Chief of Staff, would have the last word on the appointments. The shareholders of Celtic Foods Limited had bitten Mossi's hand off, albeit, that they weren't aware whose hand they'd bitten off, nor indeed did they know that the man they were dealing with was called Mossi Moscovitch as the name he was using was Saul Horowitz. None of the shareholders ever met him in person. They had just "Called Saul" when anything needed 'Breaking Bad'.

After the payment of the £50,000, to all intents and purposes Mossi was now in charge of Celtic Foods Limited. Mossi's next step was to hire people to be part of the management team. He had advertised the jobs in the Western Telegraph and he had then sifted through the applications to find the least experienced, most manipulable, ineffective people and then appointed them. Case in point was the new manager, Cledwyn Morgan. Cledwyn Morgan had played rugby for Wales and since retiring from rugby his career achievements outside of rugby had basically come from saying, "I'm Cledwyn Morgan and I played rugby for Wales." Not that these achievements had been great. He had tried sales but found negotiating and closing a sale to be difficult, if not impossible. His last job had been Deputy Manager of the Pontypridd branch of Argos. Cledwyn was 6'4" with ginger hair, cauliflower ears and a broken nose. He wore a Welsh Rugby Union blazer and tie which didn't quite fit over his expanding beer belly.

Mossi had set up another company called Dragon Foods Limited. The company, as usual, was set up with a patsy director, an Israeli student with an address of an estate agent in Brussels. Dragon Foods Limited had rented a warehouse in the outskirts of Carmarthen on a new business/retail estate. The nearest unit to the main A road was B&Q whilst Dragon Foods' warehouse sat at the far end of the estate. The unit had pre-existing storage racking and was taken under a five-year lease; the first six months of the lease were free. Dragon Foods Limited then applied to the Welsh government for a £500,000 grant on the basis that Dragon Foods Limited would be creating 250 new jobs in Wales.

After three months Celtic Foods Limited was still losing money, in fact, it was losing even more money, due to the ineffectual management team but, for now, the bank was just adding these debts to the pre-existing business overdraft. Mossi then rang Cledwyn explaining that the Ultra High Net Worth individual was intending to expand the business to twenty locations across the UK. He wanted to know though if the management team and the workforce were flexible enough to achieve this. Cledwyn replied, "We're Welsh and we have the hoyle to achieve anything," smiling to himself at this chance to prove what he could really do.

Mossi advised Cledwyn that he was very pleased to hear this as the Ultra High Net Worth individual had decided to test the management team and work force. This test of their flexibility would involve moving the staff and a day's worth of stock to a new warehouse in Carmarthen and to have it up and running in 48 hours. Cledwyn assured Mossi that this would be achieved. Mossi told him that if it wasn't heads would roll.

So it was that when the inspectors from the Welsh government visited Dragon Foods Limited in Carmarthen they would find over 250 Welsh people hard at work. The criteria for the £500,000 grant. All this worked perfectly, the grant was approved and three weeks later it was paid. The stock and the workforce were then moved back to the original warehouse. Cledwyn and his team were looking forward to the national expansion of Celtic Foods Limited. Once the £500,000 grant had been paid into the bank Mossi rang Cledwyn to advise him that the boss was so delighted with the flexibility shown by the management team and the workforce that he had given them all three days off.

Cledwyn took the opportunity to take his girlfriend Ceinwen to Tenby for a short break. Ceinwen was 5'2", slim, short black hair, pretty but with an edge such as a nose ring and tattoos adding colour to her translucent skin. Despite the sunshine she was wearing her black Doc Martins teamed with her black cut-off jeans and fishnet tights. They were sitting in the sunshine in the beer garden of the Tenby Brewery Tap. As Ceinwen ate her chowder Cledwyn looked into her eyes thinking, "Life is good" as he sipped his Tenby Harbour brewery MV Sir Galahad beer. Meanwhile the Gone Tomorrow people were loading up all of the company's stock and stripping both warehouses of the racking and every conceivable scrap of value, including the copper piping in the staff toilets.

Cledwyn returned from his break in Tenby to find disaster at Celtic Foods. They had no stock, no racking to put the stock on even if they had it and the telephone numbers and email address he had for Saul Horowitz no longer worked. He called the police and the insurance company, neither of which were that much use. The bank's view was that the company already owed them more than the liquidation of its assets would raise, therefore, they were not interested. Cledwyn had also contacted the shareholders but none of them were interested in pumping yet more money into a business they thought they had already sold. Within weeks Celtic Foods Limited had been put into liquidation and the staff, including Cledwyn, had been laid off leaving him bewildered and wondering how it had all gone so terribly wrong. Could he get a job as a picker in Argos he wondered. At least it would only be parcels going down the chute and not someone's business.

It had taken another month for the Welsh government to discover the grant fraud when a return visit had been made to Dragon Foods Limited. The Welsh government had contacted the police but the investigation had not made any progress by the time that Cassie had contacted the Welsh government and the liquidator of Celtic Foods Limited. This was in no small part due to some weeks being wasted in the decision as to whether this should be investigated by South Wales police or Dyfed-Powys police. Neither force particularly wanted the investigation. South Wales police must have had more political clout, as Dyfed-Powys police ended up with the case. Cassie contacted the Liquidator from whom she'd learned that £50,000 had been paid into the company's bank account. Cassie obtained the Liquidator's written agreement for HMRC to issue a Financial Information Notice to the company's bank in order that HMRC could follow the money. Cassie then had to wait to hear back from the bank and from HMRC's Police Liaison Officer through whom she was trying to locate the police officer dealing with the investigation of the £500,000 grant money.

The third of the companies connected to Mossi, per the Intel, was Notes in the Shower Limited. When Alan and Cassie had discussed the investigation Alan had explained the company's name to Cassie. Which was, if you want to experience what it's like to have a yacht, then stand in a cold shower tearing up £50 notes. Companies House' records showed the company to have only one director who was also the sole shareholder, a man by the name of Bill Michelin. The company's balance sheet showed that an asset had been in the balance sheet at a cost of £625,000 and had been disposed of for £1 after just two years. The company had declared a benefit in kind to Michelin of £27,500, meaning that the value of the boat when the company had sold it to Michelin for £1 was only £27,500. "Boats depreciate," thought Cassie, but £625,000 to £27,500 in two years was unbelievable. Cassie wrote to the company for the make and model and year of manufacture of the boat together with any documentary evidence in support of the valuation used to calculate the benefit in kind declared. The Company's Accountant replied, explaining that the boat was manufactured by Sunseeker, they did not know its model or year of manufacture and the reason for the large drop in value was that it had been chartered. In support of this explanation, they had provided an invoice from a marina in Mallorca. Cassie rang the marina and managed to speak to someone who could speak English. The person she spoke to was non-committal as to how long the boat had stayed at the marina and whether or not the boat had been chartered. What was on the marina's invoice was the boat's International Maritime Number. Cassie rang the Maritime and Coastguard Agency and asked if they could pull together whatever information they had for a vessel with that International Maritime Number. The Maritime and Coastguard Agency explained that this would take a few weeks but, once they had finished their search they would email over the documents they had to Cassie.

Cassie also wrote to Michelin's accountant asking for any other documentary evidence they had as to the value of the boat when it was sold, together with any documentary evidence relating to the purchase of the boat by Notes in the Shower.

CHAPTER SEVEN

Mossi already held a false passport in the name of David Goldman. It had been a long and laborious process to acquire the passport, even when Mossi had used people with experience in this field. First find a child who had died in infancy who, if he had not died, would now be about Mossi's age. Next, obtain a copy of the Birth Certificate and then fill in the documentary picture of this non-existent person's life, council tax bill, electric bill, etc. Eventually the passport was acquired.

Mossi felt the need for another false passport. He knew how to obtain one, it may not be as secure but certainly would be much quicker and cheaper.

Avi Klein was one of the little people, he did as he was told by the Rabbi and the Community Leaders. He had married Rachel when they were both sixteen, they had nine children and another one on the way. Four of their children, all boys, were registered as disabled and Avi and Rachel claimed the additional benefits due to a family unfortunate enough to have four disabled sons, in addition to the child benefits due to the nine children. Avi and Rachel weren't that unfortunate as only one of their sons was, in fact, disabled and this was the child, quite literally, wheeled out if anyone should check the claims made. Avi and Rachel were both on the payroll of Community Schools over fifty miles away, recorded as working sixteen hours a week, the sixteen hours a week was to maximise the benefits they could claim. Neither Avi nor Rachel had ever set foot in these schools let alone worked in them. They had no car and rarely travelled more than a mile or two from home. Avi did have a low paid job, cash in hand, working full time for the Solomons as an odd job man on one of the main properties in their Portfolio. Avi and Rachel also lived in a house owned by the Solomons so that the Solomons received the housing benefits that Avi and Rachel claimed from the council.

Avi had been at the same Yeshiva as Mossi and, for three years, Mossi had beaten Avi for his dinner money and anything else Mossi took a liking to. Avi was roughly the same height as Mossi and facially there were also similarities. There were, however, physical differences, Mossi's body carried a lot more muscle and Avi's eyes carried no threat, unlike Mossi's. Avi dressed and wore his hair in the Orthodox Jewish way, Mossi did not.

Rachel was tiny, barely five feet tall and very slight, aside from the bump of the next member of the Klein family she had on the way. She wore a long brown dress most of the time and her black hair was usually hidden by a scarf as she could not afford a wig.

There was a loud knock at the door, who could that be at eight o'clock in the morning? Avi put down the religious paper he had been reading, got out of his chair and went to the door. As Avi opened the door his face became a mixture of shock and fear as he saw Mossi standing in the doorway. Mossi made three movements taking little more than as many seconds. He stepped through the door, punched Avi in the solar plexus and as Avi had bent double he had brought his knee up into Avi's balls. Avi's legs had collapsed underneath him and he was now writhing on the floor. Mossi looked down at Avi both literally and figuratively as he despised Avi's lack of courage to fight back. He was a weak man, it was easy to bully him to make him bend to Mossi's will. "If only he would stand up for himself," Mossi thought. "I could still kill him but at least he would be showing some balls instead of letting me crush them with my knee." He could take anything he wanted from this man, including his self-respect, but he didn't have any to take. Obedience had been indoctrinated into him at an early age.

"Hello Klein, I've got something I want you to do for me," Mossi said in a matter-of- fact manner as he knew that Klein was already at his mercy. Rachel looked aghast at her husband on the floor. Mossi grabbed Avi by the hair and by his belt, the hair to lift him off the floor and the belt to drag him outside. Once outside Avi found his body being propelled forwards, his feet scraping along the pavement, as Mossi was still holding him off the floor by his hair. Next, he found himself in midair, before landing on the leather rear seats of the Mercedes Mossi was borrowing today. The thought passed through Avi's head, as his nose was pressed against the leather seat and hairs pulled out of his scalp tickled his right cheek, if he should ever come to own a car, even a nice car, that Mossi would probably borrow it whenever he wanted. Avi waited until the car had pulled away from the kerb before he spoke asking, "What do you want Mossi?"

Mossi had been fiddling with the aircon as he drove, being unfamiliar with the car and, until Avi had spoken, he had for the moment forgotten about him in the back. "What do I want? I want you to shut the fuck up and do as you're told, when I tell you." Avi knew better than to answer back to Mossi and so stayed stum.

Avi was still lying where he had landed on the back seat ten minutes later when Mossi told him to sit up. He obediently complied. Mossi had parked outside the Post Office. He glanced at Avi in the rear-view mirror and then at the paperwork on the passenger seat. The paperwork included photos, signed by a Rabbi four weeks ago, to be a true likeness of Avi. The Rabbi had died three weeks ago and his son with an almost identical name had taken over. Mossi had thought it highly unlikely that anyone would ever check his forgery of the Rabbi's signature. Mossi passed Avi the passport document and enough cash to pay for the passport.

"Off you go then and make the passport application, I'll wait for you here." Twenty minutes later Avi walked out of the Post Office around to the driver's side of the Mercedes, if he had been a dog he would have had his tail between his legs. With an automatic reflex, dating back to their days in the Yeshiva, he put his hand through the open driver's side window holding out the £2 change for Mossi.

"Keep it Klein, towards your bus fare home, I'll be around next month to collect my passport." Mossi laughed and with that he drove off. Avi checked his pockets and realised that his wallet was still at home and that he had a long walk ahead of him.

CHAPTER EIGHT

Mossi wasn't of course Cassie's only investigation. One of the other investigations was into Peter Philpott. He was a Director and he had been the Sole Shareholder of Newspaper Clip Limited, a technology company with no physical assets, just intellectual property. It appeared from Companies House' records that there had been a reallocation of shares in the company vastly increasing the number of shares issued, following which a substantial number of shares had been transferred to other people. Philpott had not, however, declared any capital gains to HMRC arising from the sale of these shares. In addition, the latest company accounts submitted by Newspaper Clip Ltd, showed a payment of £500,000 consultancy fees, with no indication as to whom they'd been paid or why.

Alan had agreed to Philpott being investigated under Code of Practice 9. Cassie had written to Philpott advising him that she had reason to suspect him of tax fraud. Philpott accepted the offer made by HMRC and he had admitted to committing tax frauds. Whilst his Outline Disclosure of his tax frauds included a disclosure of his failure to declare the capital gains he had made in selling shares in Newspaper Clip Ltd, there was no disclosure made regarding the £500,000 consultancy fees.

Cassie had asked for an opening meeting and this had been agreed, with the meeting to take place at the Tax Advisor's offices in London. Alan had said he would like to come along with Cassie to the meeting. This was unusual, Cassie was too experienced an investigator to even consider that Alan was coming along to check up on her, but what was his reason for attending the meeting?

Philpott's tax advisor, Thomas King, was a former colleague of Cassie's who had gone to the Dark Side. She remembered him as being about 5' 8", sandy hair, glasses, with a boyish grin, but that had been quite a few years ago now.

Most recently most people had left HMRC because HMRC had left them. Over the past 40 years the Inland Revenue and Customs & Excise had gone from having hundreds of offices across the UK to having just twelve Regional Offices. So, if you lived at Land's End, your nearest office was Bristol which wasn't a realistic commute. Cassie's former colleague though had left many years ago at which time there had been three main types of people who went to the dark side:

    a) The highflyer who had been headhunted by one of the big firms

    b) The dodgy person who had left the Department under a cloud
    c) The officer who is just not up to the job, who decided to leave rather
        than being pushed

Thomas King definitely hadn't been a high flyer and neither did Cassie think he was dodgy. From which Cassie had drawn her own conclusion as to why he had left the Department and gone to the Dark Side.

The journey from Bristol to London had been uneventful, the usual 8.30 am train from Bristol Temple Meads to London Paddington. It was fairly busy but not so much as the earlier trains to London and having reserved their seats in advance helped. Two tube journeys and a short walk brought them to the very salubrious address of Thomas King's office. Cassie and Alan stepped out of the bright sunlight and into the entrance hall of the property and Cassie introduced herself to the woman behind the reception desk. A minute later a member of staff appeared to show them to their meeting room and Cassie and Alan then went down and down and down to what must have been the basement of the basement.

"My God," thought Cassie, "this really is the Dark Side," as she wondered if King got to see the sunlight on a weekday in the winter months. Alan meanwhile had been having similar thoughts about journeying to the centre of the earth with James Mason, Pat Boone, two Icelanders and a duck. With all that boiling lava it also made Alan think of crispy duck washed down with Tiger lager.

Eventually they were shown into the meeting room and King rose to greet them. The boyish grin was still there, the sandy hair was speckled with grey but he must have put on at least five stones, thought Cassie. Philpott also rose to meet them, albeit belatedly and reluctantly. He was wearing a handmade suit and an Eton tie but his tie wasn't straight and his shoes hadn't been polished. Cassie's father had taught her that you could tell a lot about a man by looking at his shoes. Philpott's shoes suggested that he wasn't as polished as his Eton tie promised.

The meeting started ordinarily enough. Philpott provided details of his working life since leaving university, from which Cassie gathered that in a period of under two years Philpott had had five fabulous jobs on salaries she and Alan could only dream of. A Merchant Bank, a Finance House and a senior position in a government funded Quango. But the longest period Philpott had ever been in one of these jobs was five months.

He then explained that Newspaper Clip Ltd held the UK patent for an invention that was going to revolutionise the newspaper industry. Or at least that was what this chap called Chubby Smythe had told him when they met at Henley Regatta. Chubby had sold him the patent, or to be exact, had sold the patent to Newspaper Clip Ltd.

"We made £1 million sales in the first two months," Philpott boasted.

"According to the company's VAT returns those are the only sales the company has made," Cassie observed.

"Ah, yes, there have been a few teething problems," Philpott replied.

"My client's company will probably be making a substantial research and development claim in its next corporation tax return," King interjected.

"Would that be research into how to get the blooming thing to work?" Alan asked, a smile hovering on his lips as he spoke.

Philpott attempted to respond, "Well, I don't bally think…" The rest was gibberish, which to Alan's ears sounded like a conversation between Bill and Ben.

Cassie decided to move the meeting on with questions about Philpott's sales of shares in Newspaper Clip Ltd. Philpott explained that six months after he had set up the company he had begun to run out of money. He had, therefore, asked various family members and chums if they would invest in his business. The biggest investor had been his mother-in-law. He explained that his late father-in-law had died in a motor racing accident and his mother-in-law had never remarried. She was extremely rich and lived alone in Switzerland.

Alan immediately had a mental image of an older lady dressed in furs and jewels sitting at the Chemin de Fer table in the Club de Cercle asking for more credit. Beside her James Bond, having been passed a Universal Export business card, relinquished the banker's hand passing the Shoe, before collecting his considerable winnings. Alan was brought back to reality by Cassie beginning to ask Philpott about the £500,000 consultancy fees. He responded that he couldn't remember who these had been paid to or why. Cassie had just begun to ask Peter Philpott if anyone besides himself was authorised to make such a large payment from the company's bank account when, in the most dramatic way possible,

Philpott exclaimed that, "Oh my God, I've just realised I've been robbed."

There was silence in the room. Cassie glanced at King, he looked startled and then she glanced at Alan. His eyes were glinting and it was clearly all he could do to not laugh. Eventually King regained his composure and commented, "Of course we will look in detail at the £500,000 in the Disclosure Report."

Cassie had no intention of waiting for a Disclosure Report to be received, at some time in the future if she was lucky, to get Philpott's explanation of the £500,000 payment.

"I suggest you and your client look at the payment of the £500,000 in detail and that you give me a ring two weeks from today with an explanation and we can also discuss what progress you have made in kaulculating the capital gains tax arising from your client's sales of the shares." King agreed.

The remainder of the meeting was, in comparison, fairly uneventful. Philpott formally commissioned King to prepare his Disclosure Report. Cassie also asked Philpott the usual standard questions. Such as, have you received any gifts, inheritances, windfalls, lottery wins of more than £1,000? These questions were to close off bolt holes. So, for example, if six months later when Cassi asked the trader what £50,000 paid into his personal bank account related to and he replied that it was a gift from Aunt Mabel, Cassie could then point out that he had told her when they met that he had not received any gifts of more than £1,000.

Cassie also asked the standard questions to establish Philpott's assets and liabilities. Including land, properties and mortgages secured against them and also questions like:

- Do you have an aircraft, helicopter, etc?
- Do you have a racehorse?

One of Cassie's colleagues had asked a Trader do you have a boat, yacht, motor cruiser, etc? To which the Trader had replied, "No, but I do have a submarine."
There were no such replies from Philpott's answers to these standard questions and the meeting soon after came to an end. King offered to show them out.

"Good," thought Cassie, "we need a guide out of this deepest dungeon."

Alan and Cassie shook hands with King in the reception area.

"He clearly does not want to go out in the sunlight," thought Cassie. "He can return now to his troglodyte existence on the Dark Side".

As Cassie and Alan walked into the sunshine and along the pavement away from Thomas King's office and towards Hyde Park Alan said, "Chummy reminds me of the Harry Enfield character Tim-Nice-But-Dim."

Cassie was unfamiliar with the character, but Tim-Nice-But-Dim certainly fitted Peter Philpott. She imagined how Philpott had been selected for those fantastic jobs that he had.

"You know Peter, awfully nice chap, one of us you know, not bad at rugger, still plays number 8 for Eton Old Boys. Oh, what else can I tell you about Peter, oh yes, he is an awfully nice chap."

Cassie and Alan came to a street corner, Cassie was shaken from her mental wanderings by Alan informing her, "There's a really good boozer not far from here. It's called The Grenadier and offers a very passable Timothy Taylor's Landlord's best bitter."

"There it is," thought Cassie, "the reason for Alan's decision to accompany me on this particular meeting."

The Grenadier was located off Hyde Park, not far from a number of embassies and therefore had quite a select clientele including American tourists who wouldn't be disappointed with the traditional wooden bar, flooring and tables and chairs.

Cassie and Alan stood at the bar, Alan was ordering a pint of the aforementioned best bitter and a diet Coke for Cassie. Cassie knew Alan loved to mix his metaphors, nothing was ever as certain as the Pope being a Catholic or bears shitting in the woods. Alan had collected their drinks and they had found a table to sit at. The pub was fairly quiet, a few regulars at the bars and four American tourists at a table on the other side of the pub. Alan took a gulp of his pint of the Landlord's and putting his glass down on the beer mat he gave his considered opinion of Peter Philpott, "Tim-Nice-But-Dim is a picnic short of a sandwich, as certain as the Pope shits in the woods."

Alan did consider adding his response to the question, "Is the Pope a Catholic?" but he didn't do so because Cassie wouldn't remember Ian Paisley Senior. Also, Alan was of the generation that didn't joke about Ireland in public, especially in London, and he had been pushing it already with the Pope shitting in the woods. For the uninitiated the response to the question, "Is the Pope a Catholic?" is, in the best Ian Paisley Senior accent, "No, he's the antiChrist."

Twenty minutes later Alan finished his pint with an "Aaaah, Bisto!" type sound of satisfaction. After returning their glasses to the bar Cassie and Alan left The Grenadier for the tube, Paddington and home.

In contrast to the refreshing drinks and atmosphere in the pub the tube station was crowded, hot and smelly, with people anxious to get home and even more anxious not to make eye contact. Seats were reserved on the 1630 from Paddington for Cassie and Alan and, as per usual, they had to ask the two men wearing suits and ties sitting in their seats to vacate them.

After catching the 1630 from Paddington an hour had passed and Cassie looked up from her phone across at Alan in the seat opposite the railway table from her. His eyes were pinned to the sports section of the Metro then, without looking up from the newspaper, with the train rocking side to side and back and forth, Alan picked up his plastic of

Doombar, took a sip and put it back down, all without spilling a drop. "Years of experience of handling a plastic," thought Cassie. It was Shaun who had persuaded her to use the term plastic, on the basis that it wasn't a glass because it wasn't made of glass. This reminded her of a romantic city break in Prague with Shaun. After they got back from their city break she had hosted a dinner party. She was telling the girls about the architecture of Prague, its history, and their wonderful hotel, The Hotel Rott. She got up to get another bottle of wine walking past Shaun and the lads and heard him say, "And you got a beer on the plane in a real glass."

Alan finished his Doombar and was reminiscing. He said to Cassie, "I don't think I ever told you about my first knock with SCO".

"No," Cassie replied.
Alan continued, "It was a Knock on a pub. One team went in the front and another in the back. I was told I wasn't required and could stay in the car. About a minute after the team went in the front a man appeared at a small opening in the left hand side of the building, he threw something over the wall and disappeared again. I got out of the car to investigate. It was a carrier bag in which was a Simplex accounting book. I walked into the pub and found my boss flicking through a Simplex cash

accounting book. I passed him the cashbook I had found and told him he would be better off having a gander at that one. Double entry book keeping doesn't mean keeping two sets of books."

A little later Alan told Cassie another story from the days of the Inland Revenue which had happened at a Christmas party. The person in charge of the tax district was a District Inspector (DI). Within the district the DI's word was law, it was his, and occasionally her, kingdom. At the Christmas party Alan was remembering the DI was chatting to his small clique. Most of the other district staff were keeping a respectable distance away from him. The DI had just got round in and the office Union Rep, who had been standing nearby and was a little worse for wear, walked up to the DI and said, "Where's mine?" The union rep wasn't part of the clique, let alone the round. The DI dug in his pocket and gave the union rep a one-pound coin and continued the conversation within his clique.

Five minutes later the Union Rep was back, "That's not enough" he said.

"Oh really, I see," the DI replied and held out his hand to the Union Rep for the return of the one-pound coin. Which the Union Rep duly did. And then the DI boomed, "Now fuck off."

After they got back to Bristol Temple Meads Alan said his goodbyes whilst Cassie decided to return to the office to drop off the case papers before returning home.

Two weeks later Cassie got a phone call from Thomas King. He explained that following the meeting Peter Philpott had gone on holiday to the Maldives. He had, therefore, made no progress in obtaining any information in relation to whom the £500,000 had been paid. Cassie told King she would ring him in another two weeks' time for an update. The two weeks passed and Cassie rang King again as promised. She was advised that King was on annual leave until the following week. The following week Cassie was on the phone again to King. He explained that his client was on holiday in New Orleans. Cassie responded to the news that Peter Philpott was on holiday again in true Brenda from Bristol style, "Oh not another one." Whilst Cassie thought, "He's spending our money as quickly as he can." King promised Cassie that, as soon as his client was available, he would provide Cassie with the details regarding the £500,000 that Cassie had requested.

Cassie left it just one week this time before ringing Thomas King's office again. The office reception fobbed her off by saying he was in a meeting. She dug out an old case she had had with King and found what she was looking for, his mobile number. She rang the number and, as she hoped, he answered. He started waffling, she clearly caught him on the hop.

"Come on, what's going on?" Cassie demanded. That was clearly the bouncing bomb that burst the dam as the explanation came flooding out from King. It appeared that the day after their meeting Peter Philpott had himself sectioned into a mental institution. He had subsequently got worse and would continue to remain there for quite some time.

"How are we going to settle this?" asked Cassie.

King paused to think and then replied, "Let me make a few calls and then I promise I'll ring you back."

Half an hour later King rang back.

"A Tax Advisor ringing back as promised, I'd better do the National Lottery this week," thought Cassie. King had news. Philpott's wife, Pippa, had been given Power of Attorney and had appointed Thomas King to act on her behalf.

"We need to work together on this then," suggested Cassie, "let's start with the £500,000."

King began his response with, "Ah", and then explained, "the £500,000 was paid to Philpott, it was shown as consultancy but, as far as I can make out, he needed the money and used this as a way of getting the money out of the company."

"What did he need the £500,000 for?" Cassie asked.

"It was difficult to make any sense of Peter's, I mean my client's, explanation," King replied.

"Try me," Cassie responded.

King continued, "Apparently one of his old school chums owed £500,000 to a bookmaker. Reading between the lines he had been tapping up all his old friends for money and learned that one of them had just invested half a million pounds in Newspaper Clip Limited. So, he told Peter he was in fear of his life if he didn't pay the bookmaker off. Peter lent him the money but his chum couldn't resist using the £500,000 as new stake money rather than paying off his debt. Needless to say, he blew most of the money before doing a bunk and was last seen sitting at the Ice Bar in the Gala Casino in Gibraltar."

Cassie replied, "So, we have a £500,000 deduction which should be disallowed and treated as a loan to a participator, as opposed to an undeclared consultancy fee on Peter Philpott's income tax return and his failure to register this consultancy trade for VAT."

King replied, "Hmm."

"Any documentary evidence in relation to any of this?" Cassie asked.

King responded, "Nope."

"No false invoice for the consultancy income?" Cassie asked.

"No, just a journal entry," King responded.

"Oh, so it wasn't in the company records and, when the accountant prepared the company accounts, they asked, "What's this £500,000 payment?" and Peter Philpott responded "Consultancy," Cassie commented and then advised, "On a Without Prejudice basis I'm agreeable to working out the tax payable on your interpretation of the £500,000 payment as long as it is agreed that the company's behaviour was deliberate."

King responded, "Agreed".

Cassie continued, "My boss will want to know the answer to two questions: Who is going to pay? And, what is this Ice Bar in Gibraltar?"
King laughed and replied, "The Ice Bar has a strip along the bar which is kept ice cold on which you place your drinks. As to the settlement, Pippa's mother will be paying it."

"And your fees?" Cassie asked.

"Those too," King replied. What King didn't tell her was that the mother- in-law had said, "But this is the last time I am bailing him out and I'm not paying the private hospital fees this time either. It's about time my daughter divorced that man, she won't be getting any inheritance from me until she does."

Cassie ended the call by advising that she would prepare the "kaulkulations" of tax and interest due and the explanations of the penalties she intended to charge Philpott and Newspaper Clip Limited. She would email copies of these to King.

Alan agreed to King's treatment of the £500,000 and to the penalties Cassie proposed to assess, but he was most interested in The Ice Bar and commented, "No such luxury in the Donkey's Flip Flop".

"Donkey's Flip Flop?" Cassie repeated.

"The Horseshoe," Alan explained. "We had a few in there after our disappointment at the Battle of Trafalgar battlefield tour." Alan laughed and then walked away. The rest of Alan's team looked up, all of them puzzled at what Alan was laughing at, not getting the joke. A few seconds later Cassie got the joke, explaining it to the rest of the team. Not a lot to sea on the battlefield tour. Even then some of them still didn't get it, Alan's quirky humour was often cryptic.

Two months later the tax, interest and penalties had been agreed, assessed and paid. As these totalled £750,000 Alan was happy that the investigation had been brought to a successful and extremely swift conclusion, "Perhaps I should come out with you more often," Alan said.

CHAPTER NINE

It was a bright morning, the start of a new week with just a nip in the air. Cassie felt good, her run this morning had seemed almost effortless and she was more than ready to review what progress she had made with her investigation into Mossi and the companies which the Intel had linked to him. Cassie had arranged for Corporation Tax Determinations to be raised on Wheat Ear Limited as it had not submitted its Corporation Tax Returns. Wheat Ear Ltd had neither submitted these outstanding Corporation Tax Returns nor paid the Corporation Tax determined. This Corporation Tax was due and payable and, as it had not been paid, HMRC as a creditor could liquidate the company. Mary Tobin from HMRC's Fraud Investigation Service Economic Crime Section had, at Cassie's request, handled the court action leading to the liquidation of Wheat Ear Ltd and the appointment of a Liquidator. Cassie had asked Mary if, for this case, a top investigator Liquidator could be appointed.
Mary replied, "That's not how it works, you just get the next cab off the rank."

Cassie's first conversation with the Liquidator, Roy Fothergill, did not fill her with confidence. He sounded like he was in his eighties. That said, he explained that he would be appointing a solicitor to look into whether Wheat Ear Ltd had disposed of the land at undervalue. Cassie hoped that the solicitor was in his forties as opposed to being born in the forties.

On Dragon Foods and Celtic Foods Limited Cassie had issued Financial Information Notices to the banks and now had the results back. The £500,000 had been paid into the bank account of a Cypriot registered company. The £50,000, meanwhile, had come from a company registered in the Republic of Ireland. Cassie's next step was to seek authorisation of further Financial Information Notices to the banks of these two offshore companies which, fortunately, were both based in the UK so could be subject to a Financial Information Notice. These Financial Information Notices could be used to obtain the statements for the bank accounts of the Cypriot and Irish companies which could be used to follow the money. Unfortunately, the likelihood was that, having identified who had made the payments, this was likely to lead to yet another layer of money laundering. Cassie and the rest of Alan's team had seen a Powerpoint presentation that used the analogy of an onion to explain the many layers of the money laundering, used to conceal the origin of the eventual recipient of the laundered money.

When there was a break in the presentation for tea and biscuits she asked Alan what he had thought.

Alan replied, "Typical trainer sees what we do as hard work which makes you cry and leaves you with smelly fingers, we know it's a lot more fun than that. My analogy would be Pass the Parcel, there's music, there's stripping and a surprise at the end."

Cassie preferred Alan's analogy. Problem was, the music had stopped and she had stripped off a layer of the wrapping paper, but she didn't yet have the prize and had no idea how many layers there were, or if she would be able to strip them all off.

The news on Notes in the Shower Limited was somewhat better. The Maritime and Coastguard Agency had sent through their documentation which indicated that the boat was a lot larger than had previously been indicated. Also, representatives of Notes in the Shower Ltd had contacted the former Company Secretary who had copied Cassie into an email he had sent the company, attached to which was a scanned copy from a boat magazine, in which the boat had been advertised for sale for £675,000 by a company trading as a dealer selling motor cruises, yachts, etc. This company, Life on the Wave Limited, had gone into liquidation but one of its directors, Paul Avon, was now a director of Avon

On Sea Limited. Cassie googled the company who was trading as a dealer of yachts and motor cruisers, so Avon was still in the trade. Cassie rang the company and asked to speak to Paul Avon. She introduced herself as a Fraud Investigator with HMRC. She explained that she was contacting him as a third party and then she asked what records he still had from the old company's business. Avon confirmed that he had these in storage. Cassie asked when it would be convenient to come and see them and he replied, "Any time".

Cassie asked glibly, "The day after tomorrow?"

Avon agreed and asked which sale she was interested in. Cassie provided the details and Avon said, "Oh yeah, I remember that one, I will dig the file out for you and have it ready for the day after tomorrow."

The day after tomorrow turned out to be one of those unusually warm Autumn days that gets described as an Indian Summer. Cassie's drive down to the yacht brokers had been very pleasant. She had opened the sunroof on the hire car and had enjoyed the sun, the music and the relatively clear roads. She parked the car in the customer parking area and was just ringing the office to report she had arrived safely when she saw a man walking towards her car. She assumed this was Paul Avon, an assumption she discovered to be correct as she got out of the car and they introduced themselves. Avon was one of those fit yachty types, whose face wasn't so much tanned as weathered, making it difficult to decide if he was a young man who looked ten years older than he should, or an older man who looked ten years younger than he was. There was a table outside the dealership office protected on two sides by the walls of the building forming a bit of a suntrap. Avon suggested that as it was such a lovely day they sit outside to which Cassie agreed, so they sat at the table. He then popped back into the office and came out with a file half an inch thick which he placed on the table in front of Cassie.

"I can tell you quite a bit about this one," Avon explained. "It was purchased new, from Sunseeker by a local businessman. He tends to keep his motor cruisers for about three years and then replaces it with a new one. The boat was purchased for £1.2 million by a company, the Director of which was a guy called Bill Michelin. The company didn't keep up the payments on the loan it had taken out from the bank to purchase the motor cruiser and so eventually the bank repossessed it. The bank then appointed my old firm to sell it. We advertised it for sale for £675,000. We had no interest other than that from one potential company customer and this was when I met these two men representing the company, during which I discovered that one of the men was Bill Michelin."

"So they were buying back the boat that the bank had repossessed?" Cassie observed.

"Yes, but the bank didn't seem to care," Avon commented.

"What were they like, these two men?" Cassie asked.

Avon replied, "Bill Michelin was a tall chap, 6 '3" or 6' 4", balding, a bit of a beer belly, very jovial. But the other man", he paused and then continued, "have you ever seen the film Sexy Beast?" Cassie confirmed that she had. "The other man reminded me of the character played by Ben Kingsley. He exuded menace and he gave you the feeling that at any moment he might snap and, for no reason, beat you to a pulp."

"Did he give his name?" Cassie asked.

"No, and Bill Michelin referred to him, with some deference, as 'my associate'," Avon responded.

"I'd better change the subject if I want to keep him talking," thought Cassie. "What happened next to the boat?" Cassie asked.

Smiling, he replied, "The latest owners are friends of mine. They bought it for £550,000. Knowing you were coming I asked them if they could email me the purchase invoice." Avon pulled out his phone, found the attachment, then he used his thumb to expand the image of the purchase invoice and passed his phone to Cassie so that she could see that it was Bill Michelin who had sold the boat for £550,000 to his friends. "I was just going to get myself a Diet Coke, would you like one?" Cassie agreed and, as he went into the office to get their drinks, she flicked through the file in front of her. The brochure would be really useful, she thought, all these glossy photos of what was quite clearly a large motor cruiser and not one worth £27,500.

So, when Avon returned with her drink, she gave him a handwritten receipt for the file and her business card asking that he email his friend's Purchase Invoice to her email address on the card.

Avon's phone rang, he gave his apologies and said goodbye to Cassie as he walked away, already giving his sales patter to the potential customer on the phone. Cassie sipped her Diet Coke. Away from the sun trap in which she was sitting there was a slight breeze, which created an almost melodic rattling of the halyards against the masts of the yachts in the dealer's yard.

"I get paid to do this," Cassie thought.

The next day Cassie prepared a Tax Evasion Referral to Criminal Investigations in respect of Bill Michelin as he had declared a Benefit in Kind of £27,500 on a boat he had purchased from his company for £1 and then sold for £550,000. Two weeks later Criminal Investigations rejected the case, insufficient resource was given as the reason, and the suspected tax fraud was passed to Alan's team. Cassie had asked Alan if she could work the case under Code of Practice 9 but Alan had refused, citing that she had enough cases already. One of Cassie's colleagues would, therefore, be writing to Bill Michelin advising him that HMRC had reason to suspect him of tax fraud.

Cassie hadn't quite given up and said to Alan, "If you get a meeting with Michelin I want to sit in".

"This would be a good year to buy me a Pirelli calendar, I never tire of those," Alan replied. One of Cassie's colleagues, Bob, sat two desks away, laughed without looking up from his work, while his neighbour, Jim, rolled his eyes. Cassie, too focused on getting what she wanted missed the puns but took Alan's reply as a yes and, feeling that she was on a roll, she pushed on with a theory she had been investigating for a few weeks. "Do you remember that case I had a few years ago where there was a UK based brother and a USA based brother and the UK based brother had been purchasing property using the US brother's name as opposed to his own? Of course, neither brother had declared the rents received from the properties, but the UK based brother coughed when we started investigating his US based brother." Alan nodded. "Well, I wondered," Cassie continued, "if the same thing might be happening with Mossi. The house Mossi lives in is owned by a company, the Director of which is a Yeuhdah Rosenthal. I have had a search made of the Valuation Office system which shows eight properties purchased in the name of Yeuhdah Rosenthal. The last Self-Assessment Tax Return submitted by Yeuhdah Rosenthal was over ten years ago. It showed a small amount of self-employment income from a trade as a shoe repairer. The notes to the Self-Assessment Tax Record show that, around ten years ago, Yeuhdah's contact address changed from a UK address to one in New York. Companies' House records show Yeuhdah as the Director of eight UK companies, all of which are property investment companies and all of which have accounts prepared by Nigel Greenfield & Co.

"Fiction section of the library then?" Alan commented.

Cassie continued, "There are no properties registered in the name of any of these eight companies and, using figures in the accounts of the money borrowed from the banks to purchase these eight properties, there is an £800,000 shortfall in the difference between the purchase price of the properties and the mortgages taken out against them. Equifax shows eight mortgages in Yeuhdah's name and no mortgages taken out by any of the companies.

"We know what Nigel Greenfield will say," Alan commented.

Cassie smiled and said, "Here is a Trust Document showing that the property was purchased by Yeuhddah in trust for the company. With the ink still wet and miraculously never shown to anyone such as Land Registry or the mortgage lender who part funded the purchase." Cassie continued, "The big question remains, who funded the £800,000? Not from a shoe repairman's profits I think."

"He could be well heeled" Alan joked.

Cassie had nearly finished so she carried on, "I have asked the Exchange of Information team to request that the IRS provide Yeuhdah Rosenthal's US tax returns." Alan nodded in agreement. "The best bit though," Cassie beamed, "is that one of the companies is called **MM Properties Limited**. Just what you call a company when your initials are YR. What do you want to bet that the property held in trust for MM Properties is the one that Mossi Moscovitch lives in?"

"That would be nice, it's the sort of thing that sticks in a jury's mind. I agree, Motsi Mabuse, or whatever his name is, is worth looking into further. Let me know how you get on," Alan said decisively.

CHAPTER TEN

Alan decided not to give the Bill Michelin investigation to Cassie as she had enough investigations to be getting on with. One of these investigations was into the directors of a Biotech company. The directors were Clive Harrington and his wife Angelina. Their company, Bio-Tech Inventions (UK) Limited had an annual turnover of £5 million, but this consisted of two sales. So only two sales invoices were issued, one for £3 million and the other for £2 million.

A routine VAT visit had been carried out to the company, during which the HMRC officer discovered that, whilst the VAT on the £2 million sales invoice had been declared by the company, the VAT on the £3 million sales invoice had not. When the HMRC officer questioned the Harrington's as to why the VAT on the £3 million had not been declared, their explanation was that there had been a computer glitch. The HMRC officer had sent an Evasion Referral and, after Criminal Investigations had rejected it, the case had been passed to Alan's team. Alan had given the case to Cassie to review. They had both laughed at the computer glitch excuse given by the Harrington's.

Cassie began her review by looking at the tax returns of Clive and Angelina Harrington over the past fifteen years. Neither of them had declared much in the way of taxable income. Cassie then began to look online. Clive Harrington presented himself as Inventor and Serial Entrepreneur. Bio-Tech Inventions (UK) Ltd's website carried a pen picture of Harrington in which he listed his hobbies, which included driving his vintage Ferrari and his Facebook page had a photo of him driving a Ferrari 456 GTA in some carnival procession.

"That reminds me," thought Cassie, "this weekend is going to be dedicated to getting the carnival floats ready." Shaun, as always, would be on hand to help out and Barney had offered to help his Dad, as he did last year. Last year, a little worse for wear after a number of cans of cider, most unusually Barney had opened up to Cassie. From what she could make out from what Barney had said during his cider induced explanation, he had really loved working with his Dad and the other men. It had been real grown-up work, not like school with stupid algebra questions about X and Y.

Barney had then said, "Why do I need to know about Y?" before giggling uncontrollably at his unintentional joke. Cassie had managed to get out of Barney that, to him, the best bit had been that, after all the work had been completed, the men had sat around drinking beer and talking about 'man' things like football and cars and he had been sat there with the other men. He had thrown his arms around Cassie hugging her, saying, "I'll be a man soon Mummy".

Cassie had loved that chat, it was the last time Barney had called her Mummy. Part of her hoped that this year Barney might have another drunken heart to heart with her. Just as long as she didn't have to clean up Barney's vomit in the bathroom again. Cassie shook the unpleasant thought from her head and looked at Bio-tech Inventions (UK) Limited's website again. It proudly boasted that the company's new product would change the world for the better. The more Cassie researched the more interesting this investigation looked. Clive Harrington, the so-called Inventor and Serial Entrepreneur, had actually only invented one product fifteen years ago which had taken off but had subsequently ceased production. Harrington mainly appeared to receive consultancy fees for promoting other people's ideas. Nor was he above promoting other people's inventions as his own.

Cassie carried out a review of the accounts of the previous companies of which Clive Harrington had been a director. These showed payments of

Consultancy Fees far in excess of what he had declared on his tax returns. Cassie's check of any Intel connected to these companies revealed intelligence reports, most likely from UK based banks, indicating that monies had been paid in amounts similar to the consultancy fees in the accounts of the companies connected to Harrington, being paid into bank accounts in Malta and Cyprus.

Cassie recommended in her review investigating the Harrington's under Code of Practice 9 and Alan had agreed to her recommendations.

The opening letters were sent out and The Harringtons had replied admitting that they had committed tax fraud by not declaring the VAT on the £3 million sales invoice issued by Bio-Tech Inventions (UK) Ltd. They explained that they had done so due to cash flow reasons and had no intention of not paying the money owed. Despite Cassie requesting a payment on account, against the VAT owed by the company, none had been made and The Harrington's explained the company didn't have the money to pay it. Put simply, Bio-Tech Inventions (UK) Ltd had charged its customer VAT and, rather than declaring it and paying it to HMRC, the money had been used to pay the company's debts and to make payments to Clive and Angelina Harrington. A date was arranged for a meeting with the Harrington's at what was described as Bio-Tech Inventions (UK) Ltd's UK Headquarters.

Cassie travelled to the company HQ with her colleague Carl. Carl was by far the best note taker for an opening meeting. Cassie marvelled at how much detail Carl managed to get into the notes of a five-hour meeting. When Cassie and her colleague Carl arrived at the address provided for the company's UK headquarters, it was somewhat of a surprise. Particularly for a company that was going to change the world. It was a small office in a farmyard. Cassie's first reaction was to regret her choice of footwear, welly boots would have been a better choice than high heels. Having negotiated muddy puddles and got into the office relatively unscathed, Cassie looked around. There was no lab, unless you counted the one with the waggy tail sat by a calor gas heater. The office looked disorganised and there was no indication that this was the offices of Bio-Tech Inventions (UK) Ltd or, in fact, any Biotech company.

Cassie and Carl introduced themselves to Clive Harrington, Angelina Harrington and their Tax Advisor, Bob Knowles. Clive Harrington looked nothing like a scientist. Cassie hadn't exactly expected a lab coat and glasses, but a shirt undone at least two buttons too far and a gold sovereign on a chain around his neck was a surprise. She looked again, he was, he was wearing make-up. Not for any LGBTQ+ reason, but for the simple reason that he was extremely vain.

This reminded Cassie of another extremely vain man she had met years ago. She had been visiting an accountant's office to have a look at the business records in support of a trader's VAT returns prepared by this accountancy firm.

Some accountants like to play mind games by keeping you waiting. Cassie had found the best solution was always to take a book to read. That way when the accountant eventually came out, after deliberately keeping them waiting and disingenuously said, "Sorry for keeping you waiting," Cassie could reply, "That's okay, this is such a good book." And, if the accountant had kept her waiting a long time, she could add, "Do you mind waiting a sec, this is a good bit and I just want to get to the end of the page."

On this occasion there hadn't been much delay and, when the accountant saw Cassie, his face lit up and he was charming to an almost creepy degree. The accountant, Christopher Jenkins, was in his mid-fifties, his hair looked like it was cut and coloured weekly, his suit was made to measure, shirt, tie and matching hanky immaculate and his skin was shiny from the regular use of moisturiser. His shoes were polished but looked at first to Cassie to be somewhat odd, until she realised they had hidden insteps and even with these Jenkins was only 5' tall. After Jenkins had shown Cassie to the room where the business records were set out for her, he had left her to it. Cassie had been offered a cup of coffee by one of Jenkins' staff and later she had needed to ask another member of staff where the ladies loo was. When Cassie had asked to photocopy some of the business records she had met two more of his staff and it had struck Cassie that his members of staff were all good looking women. In fact, Jenkins had ten members of staff, all were women and none of them were over forty. By lunchtime Cassie had finished what she needed to do and was just about to leave when Jenkins came out of his office, flung his Louis Vuitton sports bag over his shoulder and said, in a voice clearly meant to impress Cassie and any other female in earshot, "I'm off to the gym now."

"Would you like tea or coffee?" asked Clive Harrington, bringing Cassie back to today's very vain man and the farmyard office, UK Headquarters of Bio-Tech Inventions (UK) Ltd. Cassie accepted a black coffee and, once hers and the other drinks arrived, she got the meeting started. The questions regarding VAT on the £3 million sales invoice didn't take long. Both Clive and Angelina Harrington admitted they were the Company Officers responsible for Bio-Tech Inventions (UK) Ltd's VAT returns and that they had acted deliberately and fraudulently in submitting the company's VAT return without declaring the VAT on the £3 million sales invoice. The company's accountant, Bob Knowles from Simpkin & Knowles, stressed that his clients admitted that they had acted deliberately, but they had done so due to cashflow reasons and they had intended to rectify this data. This was proved, he explained, by the fact that the Directors had submitted company accounts and Corporation Tax Return which declared both the £2 million and the £3 million sales invoices.

"Your point is?" Cassie asked Knowles. Knowles waffled a bit about all accountants would obviously prepare accounts including both the £2 million and £3 million sales invoices.

"You clearly don't know Nigel Greenfield" Cassie thought. Knowles then got to answering Cassie's question, "It wasn't concealed because the company declared both sales in its accounts."

"Deliberate but not concealed then?" Cassie asked. Knowles nodded.

Cassie turned to Clive Harrington and asked, "Why has the company not paid the VAT it owes?" Harrington started talking about how the company's product would change the world and the conversation he was having with potential major investors.
Cassie stopped him mid-sentence when he started talking about projected sales for the next three years and she asked, "How much money does the company have in the bank as of today's date?" Harrington mumbled something about cash flow.

"Is a patent held for this product the company is promoting?" Cassie enquired.

"Not as yet," Harrington replied.

"These are rented offices aren't they?" Cassie guessed and the Harringtons confirmed.

"Does the company have any assets which could be sold to pay its debts?" The Harringtons didn't respond but both looked at Bob Knowles with hope. Cassie turned to Knowles and said, "I have reason to believe the company is insolvent. Mr and Mrs Harrington have admitted they acted deliberately and were the officers of the company responsible for the incorrect VAT return. I shall therefore be issuing a VAT assessment, penalties and Personal Liability notices."

Clive Harrington turned to Bob Knowles and asked, "What does that mean?" Knowles replied, "HMRC will assess tax and penalties payable by the company and if the company can't pay, yourself and Angelina will be liable to pay the penalties personally." Clive Harrington opened his mouth as if to speak but no sound came out. Cassie moved on to look at the personal tax affairs of Clive and Angelina Harrington. She began by getting Clive Harrington to talk about his favourite topic of conversation, himself. Cassie already knew that he had invented a type of Thermos flask which wouldn't break if you dropped it and she already knew that the money he had made from this invention, 15 years ago, had been declared. What she wanted to know was what he had done subsequently and what monies he and his wife had taken out of Bio-Tech Investments (UK) Ltd. Clive Harrington had an eight-year gap in his personal tax returns when HMRC had stopped issuing tax returns to him and Harrington hadn't notified HMRC that he was liable to tax. This had ended when he became a director of Bio-Tech Investments (UK) Ltd five years ago. HMRC had started sending Tax Returns again, but he hadn't submitted them and he currently had three years of Tax Returns outstanding. Cassie asked Clive Harrington about his pen picture on the company's web site which described him as an Inventor and Serial Entrepreneur. Harrington described how he had invented his flask and later sold the business. Then as a proven Inventor and Entrepreneur he had been working with some major companies developing and promoting their products and, when Cassie showed an interest, he began to reel off the names of the companies and their products.

Cassie then asked, "So did you invest your own money in these products like the Dragons on Dragons' Den?"

"Oh no," Harrington replied, "I was paid as a consultant". Realising the trap he had fallen into, Harrington responded to the remainder of Cassie's questions on his undeclared consultancy income over the past eleven or twelve years with, "We'll have to check." He might just as well have said, "No comment."

Cassie asked Angelina Harrington how long she had been married and where they had met, from which Cassie gained the useful information of Angelina Harrington's maiden name and the fact she was from Malta, which fitted with the Intel of Clive Harrington using an offshore account in Malta.

Cassie later moved on to standard questions asked by HMRC to establish if a Trader had any valuable assets. Which was useful to know, both to know how a Trader had funded the purchase of the asset and how much the sale of the asset would raise to pay the tax the trader owed. Clive Harrington's "No comment" type responses continued in relation to these standard questions. For example, when Cassie asked, "Do you have or have you had in the past ten years a sports car or classic car?" Harrington replied, "No".

"Do you have a Ferrari or have you had a Ferrari in the past ten years?"

Harrington replied, "No".

Cassie asked, "On the company's website it says one of your past times is driving your Ferrari and on your Facebook page are photos of you driving a Ferrari GTA."

Harrington replied, "Oh, that Ferrari."

The meeting continued without much incident and a continuation of the "We'll need to check" responses with assurances from Bob Knowles they would do just that. Cassie advised Knowles that she would give him a ring in two-weeks' time for an update on all of this.

The meeting ended with the usual pleasantries. Cassie and Carl left the company's UK Headquarters and its lab, sitting in front of the calor gas heater.

The next day Cassie began the paperwork on the VAT Assessment and by the end of the week the VAT Assessment, penalties and Personal Liability Notices were issued.

A further week went by and, not having heard from the Harringtons or their Tax Advisors, Cassie gave Bob Knowles a ring. Cassie was advised that he was in a meeting. The next day she rang again and got the same response. Not having his mobile number and having emailed him without receiving a response Cassie decided to ring at 17.45 working on the basis that, if Knowles was still in work, it was likely that whoever had been shielding his calls would have gone home. Cassie was in luck and got through to him. Cassie asked him how things were going, to which Knowles replied, "We are no longer acting."

"What already?" Cassie said. "What happened, did the cheque bounce?"

Knowles' silence told all before he commented, "Not much call for cheques these days."

"No, just bank transfers made with insufficient funds," Cassie commented. "Did you get any additional information from the clients?" she continued.

"Oh, lots of information, but none that will help you with your investigation," Knowles replied.

"Let me guess, potential investors lining up around the farmyard," Cassie commented. Knowles chuckled and then said goodbye.

Cassie rang Clive Harrington the next day. He gave the same answer that they would need to check in relation to the outstanding information. He confirmed that they had no Tax Advisor as he had decided that he could deal with this himself. And, of course, there were people wanting to invest in the company so everything will be okay soon. Cassie saw little point in asking when and from whom this investment money was going to be received. She instead explained that she would today be issuing a formal information notice to Clive Harrington requiring him to provide the documents and information she required to assess his undeclared consultancy fees.

"What if we can't find the consultancy fee information?" Harrington asked.

"Then I will have to raise assessments using my best judgement," Cassie replied.

"Well, I will appeal," Harrington said with confidence.

"If you can't find the consultancy fee information, how would you convince a judge that my best judgement assessments are incorrect?" Cassie asked. Being his own Tax Advisor wasn't as simple as he thought and without a response to Cassie's question, Clive Harrington pressed the button on the phone ending the call.

Cassie received no response to the Information Notice and, after receiving Alan's authorisation issued an initial penalty of £300, Cassie sent the £300 penalty out with a covering letter to Clive Harrington in which she explained the adverse effect his continued lack of cooperation could have on any penalties assessed in future, in respect of his failure to declare the consultancy fees. She wanted to be able to show that she had given him every opportunity to cooperate.

A month later Cassie had already begun to charge daily penalties of £20 a day on Clive Harrington for failing to comply with the information notice when she learned that Bio-Tech Inventions (UK) Ltd had gone into liquidation. Chivers and Gilzean had been appointed as the liquidators. It was shortly after this that Cassie began to get emails from Harrington. These were unsolicited and in no way constituted a response to the Information Notice. Instead, they included what could be best described as a rant. Cassie continued to issue daily penalties with covering letters, offering to meet with Harrington or to have a conference telephone call to progress matters.

Two months after the appointment of the liquidators Cassie got a call from one of them, Gerald Gilzean who, in a tone reminiscent of the Fast Show character who always said, "You ain't seen me, right?", told Cassie that Clive and Angelina Harrington had sold their house and he had heard planned to do a runner.

Cassie lost no time in preparing the tax and penalty assessments arising from the undeclared consultancy fees. Using her best judgement and then having obtained Alan's authority to issue them, she had emailed these to Harrington but for a belt and braces approach she had decided to hand deliver them.

So that morning she and Carl were off to do just that. As Carl drove, Cassie recalled another occasion when they had travelled together. Carl had driven and she had agreed to navigate, as the Satnav wasn't working. Their destination had been Bicester, which Carl pronounced By-ces-terr, rather than Bister. As they had got outside Bristol and Cassie had begun to try to navigate, she realised she didn't have her driving glasses to read the road signs, nor did they have a map.

This time the Satnav was working and Cassie's driving glasses were in her handbag just in case. They weren't needed, however, and they arrived at the beautiful thatched cottage the Harringtons had called home. The past tense being indicated by the removal van outside. The front door was open and there was a small table in the hallway on which, post had been placed. Cassie added the envelopes containing her assessments to the pile. She had briefly considered knocking on the door so that as she put them in Clive Harrington's hands she could say, "You've been served," in the American style, but decided that this was more British in style akin to "All because the lady loves Milktray" and, furthermore, was less likely to lead to a confrontation and the inevitable complaint that would follow. As she turned away Cassie did have a Schadenfreude thought of Clive Harrington crying and his mascara running.

Cassie took a pen and notebook from her jacket pocket and noted down the name, address and telephone number of the removal firm, as well as the vehicle registration mark of the lorry. She then went to speak to the driver and asked him, "Where are they off to?"

"Italy," the driver replied.

The next day Cassie rang the removals firm and asked to speak to the Managing Director. When the Managing Director, Brandon Beal, came on the line Cassie said, "Hello, my name is Cassie Holmes-Smith. I'm a fraud investigator with HMRC. I am contacting you regarding a removal you are undertaking. I realise that I am phoning you out of the blue, but I am happy to drive down today to show you my proof of identity with HMRC."

"Oh, I am sure that won't be necessary," Brandon replied.

"If you could give me your email address, I can email you and you can at least see that I am emailing you from a government address," Cassie explained.

Brandon provided his email address and Cassie sent him a test email.

"What do you want to know?" Brandon asked.

Cassie provided Brandon with the vehicle registration mark of the lorry and the date of the collection and explained that she wanted to know the destination the furniture was being delivered to.

"I think that we can do better than that," Brandon said.

True to his word, two days later Cassie received an email from Brandon with, not only the address of the property in Italy to which the furniture had been delivered, but also a Google Maps reference which enabled Cassie to bring up a photo of the property.

Cassie contacted the Mutual Assistance for the Recovery of Debt Team. This team dealt with countries such as Italy with whom HMRC had an agreement, whereby HMRC could transfer its debts to the Italian tax authorities and the Italian tax authorities would then retain what tax they collected. There was obviously a reciprocal arrangement in relation to monies owed to the Italian tax authorities by people living in the UK. Cassie provided the details of Clive Harrington's debt to the Italian tax authorities, together with the address in Italy to which the furniture had been delivered.

Cassie would have liked Clive Harrington in his Ferrari 456 GTA to meet a similar end to the Lamborghini Miura in the opening scene of The Italian Job, but she would settle for the Italian debt collectors knocking on his door.

Strangely, this wasn't the last that Cassie would hear from Clive Harrington as, for reasons best known to himself, he had continued to email Cassie. In the last email she had received from him he stated that he was travelling, staying with friends as he had no money and he was trying to find himself. "Don't worry", Cassie thought, "I have already found you."

CHAPTER ELEVEN

It was cold this morning and Cassie had a hot water bottle on her lap before she had even logged on. She checked her email inbox. Cassie's emails fell into certain categories:

a) Mark as, read later. This included emails that Alan had received and passed on to the team who may be interested. These never included emails on pink and fluffy subjects, having already been consigned to Alan's deleted bin.

b) Emails deleted on sight. These usually included;

   i) Emails sent to the world and his wife, irrespective of whether the recipient had any need or requirement to receive the information they contained,

   ii) Emails from senior management, along the lines of 'Are You Being Served' Young Mr Grace's speech, "You've all done very well," which would usually create the response from Alan's team of, "Great, can we have a pay rise then?"

- iii) Pink and fluffy emails, where her email address was on the address list and so hadn't already been cut out by Alan.

c) Lastly, emails she was actually waiting for.

Today in Cassie's in box was one such email. It was from the Exchange of Information Team passing on a response from the IRS with copies of Yeheudah Rosenthal's US tax returns. The US tax returns were interesting more for what they didn't show than what they did. Yeheudah had declared he had no income from outside of the USA, he had no interest in any companies outside the USA and the income he had declared was nowhere near enough to explain how he could have possibly funded the purchase of eight properties in London. What Yeheudah had declared was a very small profit from his self-employed trade as a repairer of shoes.

Cassie rang the manager of the Exchange of Information team, Brian England, who she had worked with before as she wanted to make an unusual request. Having chatted briefly about the case that she and Brian had worked on before, Cassie explained the background to her new case and her suspicion that the properties purchased in Yeheudah Rosenthal's name actually belonged to Mossi. She then made her request that simultaneous enquiries into Yeheudah's tax affairs be made by HMRC and the IRS on the basis that he couldn't tell HMRC that he was the director of eight companies and tell the IRS that he wasn't. Brian England asked Cassie to set out her reasons for the request in a document and he could then use this as part of his request to the IRS. Brian added that Cassie's request had the advantage that hers would be only the second such request made by HMRC to the IRS. "I know I can sell this to the IRS," thought Cassie, "it would've been nice though to be the first simultaneous enquiry to the IRS, or should that be an inquiry? Even so, this is how we are going to break this case."

Cassie got to work on the document that would sell the simultaneous suggestion to the IRS. Those emails she had marked as read later would have to wait.

A couple of days later Cassie had emailed Brian her documents in support of the simultaneous enquiry request and she was about half way through reading the emails she had marked as read later. She had decided to give herself a break and had just got back to her desk with a black coffee when the phone on her desk rang. After establishing her identity the caller identified himself as John, the son of the person she had appointed as liquidator of Wheat Ear

Limited. John said, somewhat breathlessly, "Last night Mum and Dad were in bed when, about 1 am, three masked men burst into their bedroom. They dragged them from their bed and stood them up against the wall and, whilst two of them held Mum and Dad by their throats, the third was emptying a Jerry Can of petrol over the bed and bedroom furniture. Before setting light to the petrol one of the men said to my Dad, 'If you don't stop your investigation of Wheat Ear Limited next time we will roast you alive, this is your last warning and that goes for the tax woman too.'"

"How are your Mum and Dad?" Cassie asked. "Still in shock" John replied, "they've moved and Dad has promised Mum he has now retired. I don't think they'll ever move back in, although they couldn't do so even if they wanted to as a major part of the house will need to be rebuilt due to the fire damage."

"Have they told the Police?" asked Cassie. John confirmed that they had and at present, Scene of Crimes Officers were searching the rooms of the house.

Cassie felt guilty that she had caused this to happen to this innocent old couple. She went over to Alan's desk and told him what had happened. Alan said,

"Wait there a sec," and returned with two lead crystal tumblers and a bottle of ten-year old Laphroaig single malt. Alan poured them both a double measure and got Cassie to open up about how she was feeling. She felt guilty, but no way did she want to give up the investigation by asking Alan to transfer it to someone else. Alan assured her he had no intention of transferring it to anyone else. If Cassie no longer wished to continue with it, which would be fully understandable, he would run it himself. "Let's work it together, but I insist you tell your family. Obviously, no names, no pack drill," Alan said.

Cassie agreed and then needed a visit to the Ladies. By the time she was walking back to her desk she was feeling a bit better and guilty thoughts had been replaced by her usual investigative mind. "How on earth, in these days of hot desking and small lockable containers for personal items, let alone a no alcohol policy in the building, did Alan manage to magically produce a bottle of single malt whisky and two glasses?"

When Cassie got home she told Shaun the gist of what had happened. She then shouted up the stairs to tell Wendy and Barney they were needed in the kitchen. Wendy and Barney both recognised from the tone of their Mum's voice that they'd better come downstairs and hear what she had to say. When they were all present Cassie announced, "We're coming off all Social Media."

Shaun glanced at his watch and then replied, "Is that it? Liverpool are kicking off in the Champions' League in half an hour and I'm meeting a couple of lads at the pub to watch it." Cassie smiled at Shaun and his priorities. Shaun took this as a yes and was already putting his jacket on.

Barney would have loved to have joined his Dad at the pub but, failing that, he had just reached the last level of his new computer game, so he shrugged his shoulders and was back off to his Man Cave.

Cassie looked at Wendy and could see she was mentally preparing her arguments. Cassie preempted this, "Let's have a cup of tea." Over the cup of tea Cassie explained to Wendy what had happened to the liquidator and his wife. "You see," Cassie explained, "if the bad guys can trace me and my family, the same could happen to us and that's why we must come off all Social Media now."

Wendy didn't reply, she was thinking hard to formulate a response as to why for her to give up Social Media was just not fair. But each response she formulated sounded petty and childish compared to her Mum's desire to prevent her family from being threatened and their house burnt down. Eventually, having failed to formulate an argument which would enable her to have her own way, which was in itself a very rare occurrence, she decided she would at least have the last word. "Why couldn't you just have been a Social Worker?" And with that Wendy was gone.

Cassie replied to a now empty kitchen, "Because, unlike all the social workers I've ever met, I'm not in need of a social worker myself."

Sandy Williams watched the hundreds of little hermit crabs clawing their way up the beach. When she had first seen these crabs on the beach at Cavelossim in Goa, she had thought that they were shingle and she had to look twice as she thought she was seeing things, because the shingle appeared to be moving in the opposite direction to that which you would have expected. She enjoyed her early morning walk along the beach, before the sun got too high in the sky and whilst it was still reasonably cool. Trotting behind her was a small black beach dog she had named Shadow, his coat already beginning to shine from the regular meals he had been receiving from Sandy. He already had his own bowl in the kitchen of the small flat Sandy had been renting. Sandy adjusted the sarong she wore over her bikini; she had purchased it from one of the Indian girls on the beach, who went by the name of Mary. That was a week ago and already at least half of the sequins on the elephant motif had fallen off. She didn't mind though as those girls worked so hard and she marvelled at how they spoke in English one minute and in Russian the next. She was, however, being careful with her money as she had to be relatively frugal with the money she had brought with her. In Goa she hoped it would last her quite some time. Ten days ago she had heard about the liquidator being threatened by masked men who had set fire to his house. She had told Cliff, the farmer next door, that her sister in California was ill in hospital and asked if he would accept her dog and her donkey as a gift as she had no idea when she would be back. She knew he was a kind man who would look after them. Cliff was a bachelor, in his forties who even his fellow farmers in the pub on market day would avoid because he could bore for England. Sandy knew that Cliff fancied her and she felt certain that she could be gone for a couple of years and he would still be looking after her animals for her. With her mind at peace over the care of her animals, she decided on Goa as a beautiful place to disappear to for a while, where she could live fairly cheaply. Since she had arrived in Goa she had been delighted with her choice of escape destination. She was already this morning looking forward to lunch at one of the beach shacks, a spring roll, or some dahl and paratha, washed down with a cold glass of Kingfisher lager. An expense on her tight budget, but one she justified on the basis that this was an investment in her search for a new man.

She had begun her search at the beach hut outside what appeared to be the most expensive hotel. This had been her first day on the beach but she had found that most of the clientele were Russian. There were families and couples, children with both Mum and Grandma. She had seen a few single men but they appeared to have brought their girls with them and Sandy recognised girls from her former profession when she saw them. Since then she had divided her lunches between the beach shacks by the Holiday Inn and the Dona Sylvia hotels. Yesterday when she was walking towards a shack called Silver Springs at about 1pm she had seen a man walking alone, away from the shack and into the hotel grounds. So, today her plan was to be sitting in the Silver Springs beach shack by noon in the hope he would lunch there again and she could get to meet him. At that moment a cow emerged from the woodland beside the beach and walked across and into the sea in front of Sandy. She took this to be a good omen for her chances of meeting a new man this lunchtime. She smiled and thought to herself, "Mossi who?"

Meanwhile, in a grey and overcast Bristol, Cassie's colleague Debbie had opened a Code of Practice 9 investigation into Bill Michelin sixty-two days ago. Debbie would be checking her emails this morning to see if Michelin had admitted to the tax fraud within the sixty-day time limit and if he had disclosed the tax frauds of which he was suspected.

The tax fraudster was required to provide their admission of tax fraud and their outline disclosure within 60 days of the opening letter. If the outline disclosure was not acceptable it would be rejected.

Cassie had never understood why most tax advisors submitting their client's outlined disclosure of their tax frauds waited until day sixty before doing so. It wasn't unusual, for example, for an Outline Disclosure to be submitted which was not acceptable to HMRC, but which would be with some small amendment. If, of course, the Outline Disclosure was submitted on day sixty and this fell on a weekend, or on a day when the investigating officer was on leave, there would be no time to amend it before the sixty days expired.

Debbie's review had identified that Michelin had undeclared rents and undeclared capital gains made from the sale of two properties. Fortunately for Michelin, when his Outline Disclosure was received it was acceptable and included all the tax frauds of which he was suspected. He had admitted that he had deliberately under-declared the Benefit in Kind arising from his purchase of the boat from Notes in the Shower Limited for a pound. He had also admitted to deliberately not declaring the rent he had collected from the two properties and the capital gains he had made from the sale of these two same properties. It had, therefore, appeared that Michelin had made a full disclosure of his tax frauds. So this, therefore, should be a relatively straightforward investigation. The next step would be to hold an opening meeting with Michelin at which he would be asked to confirm his Outline disclosure and to appoint a Tax Advisor to prepare his Disclosure Report. The Disclosure Report would then quantify how much tax he owed to HMRC.

This confirmation of an Outline Disclosure of the Trader's tax frauds was in no way guaranteed. Many a Trader happily signed documents in the Tax Advisor's office admitting his or her tax fraud, but when questioned about it face to face by officers of HMRC at an opening meeting, then started to provide excuses:

- "It's all a big mistake"
- "It's all my Tax Advisors fault"
- "My former Tax Advisor colluded with HMRC"
- "I just signed what my husband put in front of me"
- "It wasn't me, it was my brother"

Cassie's personal favourites:

- "I felt pressured by HMRC into admitting the tax fraud"

Cassie's thoughts on which were, "Sorry, that's the whole bloody point."

- "My client is suffering from depression"

Cassie's thoughts on which were, "No shit Sherlock, you've been caught, big surprise, you are depressed."

Best of all was a reason a Trader had once given for the Outline Disclosure being late, "Our Alsatian dog got his tongue trapped in the fax machine."

A date was arranged for the opening meeting with Bill Michelin. Debbie, Carl and Cassie would be attending for HMRC. Bill Michelin would be represented by Wilfred Jennings, of Neighbour & Jennings, at whose offices the meeting was to take place.

The day of the opening meeting arrived and Debbie, Carl and Cassie travelled by train to Portsmouth where Neighbour & Jennings' offices were located. The three HMRC officers then got a taxi to the offices of Neighbour & Jennings which was not far from the site of the original Joanna's Nightclub.

Cassie's Dad had told her tales of Joanna's. Such as the classic palm trees in Joanna's, like those in the lyrics of the song by the Leyton Buzzards.

"Saturday nights beneath the plastic palm trees, dancing to the rhythm of the guns of Navarone."

Or the time her Dad had been dancing with a girl, in Joanna's and then had gone to the bar just because he fancied a pint. Only to see the next bloke who danced with her being beaten to a pulp and, for good measure, thrown out of the nightclub by her bouncer boyfriend.

The offices of Neighbour & Jennings looked like they were stuck in the 1970s along with the Leyton Buzzards. The waiting room contained a large painting of HMS Victory and the walls, coloured nicotine brown, were covered with ships' plaques and black and white photos of war ships. Cassie wondered when the walls were last painted. How long ago was it that smoking had been allowed in accountants' waiting rooms? Cassie wandered around looking at the photos of the ships, they looked ancient. The most recent appeared to be HMS Fearless. Which reminded Cassie of her Dad. Whenever he met someone who claimed to be a James Bond fan he would ask them, "Who sang the closing credits of The Spy Who Loved Me?"

The Bond fan would reply, "Carly Simon". To which her Dad would reply, "No, I did" and after a pause, "and the rest of the crew of HMS Fearless."

Cassie was still looking at the photo when the door opened and a man with a stoop and straggly white hair said, "Please come this way." Cassie and her colleagues followed him. Cassie was reminded of Tommy Steele in a stage performance she had seen at the Bristol Hippodrome of The Glen Miller Story. Tommy Steele was playing Glen Miller who, at the time, was in his twenties. Tommy Steele meanwhile was shuffling with a stoop and in every dance number a piece of furniture or stage scenery was strategically placed to prop him up. As they entered Wilfred Jennings' office a large man, who introduced himself as Bill Michelin, leapt to his feet to shake them each by the hand. Something Wilfred Jennings had neglected to do. Cassie thought it more likely that he had forgotten to do so, rather than him being rude. Cassie looked around the office thinking Alan would love this, there were piles of files all around Jennings' desk with clearly defined pathways for him and his clients to find their way to the chairs through the ravines of files. There was no computer to be seen and Cassie wondered who had emailed the Outline Disclosure to Debbie.

Michelin was just as Paul Avon had described him, large in size and personality. He was dressed like the Commodore of a yacht club, blazer, trousers, shirt, tie and deck shoes. No refreshments were offered and Jennings just said, "Shall we get on?" Michelin looked a little surprised at the sudden start to the meeting and Cassie wondered if offering tea and coffee was another thing Wilfred Jennings had forgotten to do.

Debbie began to ask the questions she had for Bill Michelin in their interview brief, Carl was writing furiously, getting every detail down. Cassie, meanwhile, made the occasional note but spent most of her time studying Michelin's reactions to Debbie's questions. Michelin confirmed the details in the Outline Disclosure of his tax frauds. He answered all of Debbie's questions on this subject with the air of a man who has resigned himself to being hit with a big bill. Which was funny given he was a big Bill himself. Debbie moved on to standard questions about relationships and children. Michelin confirmed he was, as he put it, "Happily divorced." And in answer to the question, "Do you have any children?" he gave the laddish reply, "Not that I know of."

This reminded Cassie of a case a colleague, Matt, had had. The Trader claimed to have no wife or children, it was his brother in Nigeria who had a wife and kids. Matt didn't believe the Trader as he thought that the brother and the Trader were one and the same person. Matt had asked to see the Trader's business records. The business records, consisting of sales and purchase invoices, were received in three cardboard boxes secured shut with gaffer tape. The advertising on the cardboard boxes showed them to have previously held Pampers' nappies. Just what every single man with no children would have to hand.

Debbie had reached the section of her interview brief where she asked Michelin if he would commission a Disclosure Report. Michelin confirmed that he would and he would appoint Neighbour & Jennings to prepare it. Wilfred Jennings stated that the Disclosure Report would be completed in six months and that Michelin had today made a payment on account of £50,000. Debbie then turned to Cassie, as this was the point in the meeting where they had previously agreed at which Cassie would ask her questions. Up until this point Michelin had remained jovial particularly for a man who had just paid out £50,000 with more to follow.

Cassie began her questions by asking Michelin to confirm if she had correctly understood his description of what had happened. Michelin confirmed that Cassie was correct in her understanding, that a company of which he was a director had purchased the boat with a loan from the bank, that the company had not kept up the payments so the bank had repossessed the boat and that Notes in the Shower Limited had purchased the boat from the same bank, via a broker, at a good price.

"What was the name of the broker you dealt with?" Cassie asked.

"Paul Avon," Michelin replied, "I remember because the plastic pig, I mean the tender on the boat, was manufactured by Avon.

"Tender, plastic pig, I am not au fait with these nautical terms," Jennings commented.

"The small rubber boat with an outboard motor we use to get ashore when we are anchored off and the Gin and Tonics are running low," Michelin explained.

"Who is we?" Cassie asked.

Michelin's face had gone ashen, "Um, well it's just a figure of speech".

"If you are royalty," Cassie thought. "When you met the broker Paul Avon to discuss the price you were willing to pay for the boat. Were you on your own or was someone with you?" she then asked.

"I don't recall," Michelin replied.

"So, you remember the name of a complete stranger but you can't remember whether you were on your own or not?" Cassie stated.

"I don't recall," Michelin repeated. At this point Jennings interjected, "Where are these questions going?"

"Where I want them to go obviously," Cassie thought to herself, before retorting "Establish the facts to kaulkulate the tax." And then asking Michelin "Do you know a man called Mossi Moskovitch?"

If Michelin looked grey before, he now looked like death warmed up.
"I really need to know where these questions are going," Jennings demanded.

"I am seeking to establish if Mossi Moskovitch was a shadow director of Notes in the Shower Limited," Cassie explained, "and whether Notes in the Shower Limited sold the boat to your client alone or to him and Mossi Moskovitch. If this was the case your client would only be liable to a portion of the benefit in kind, not 100% of it."

"I am doing your job for you, what are you moaning about?" thought Cassie.

The penny finally dropped for Jennings and he asked Cassie and her colleagues, "Would you mind stepping outside so I can have a word with my client?"

The three HMRC officers picked up all of their briefs and other paperwork and moved into the corridor. Where they stood in silence. Alan had trained them well, to leave nothing behind for the other side to leave and remember, "Walls have ears, as well as sausages."

As Cassie was waiting her thoughts of a notorious tax advisor, Duncan Ramsey, came to mind. He was an ex-Revenue officer who had gone to the Dark Side. Ramsey definitely fell into the dodgy, left under a cloud category. He was renowned for dressing like a cowboy. Cassie had met him at a meeting where he was representing a Trader who had switched Tax Advisers. Ramsey had become the trader's Tax Advisor at a point in Cassie's investigation when she was looking to bring it to a conclusion and agree the sum of tax interest penalties payable by the trader. He had insisted on a meeting at HMRC's offices in Cardiff. This had caused Cassie both the hassle of arranging a room for the meeting and also car parking and security passes for her, her colleague, Ramsey and his client. True to form Ramsey turned up for the meeting wearing a cowboy hat and a leather waistcoat. His intention appeared to be to look like John Wayne, but to Cassie he looked more like Deputy Dawg. Cassie had walked down from the meeting room to the security desk so that she could escort Ramsey and his client to the meeting room. For the whole walk back, which wasn't a short one, Ramsey, or Deputy Dawg as Cassi was now minded to call him, was ranting that there hadn't been enough parking. "HMRC aren't that well prepared for a Chuck wagon and a team of horses," Cassie thought.

When they got to the meeting room, Deputy Dawg pulled out a laptop and announced, "I will be recording this meeting and you can't stop me." Cassie, following HMRC's published internal guidance, requested that Deputy Dawg provide her with a copy of the recording to which Deputy Dawg replied, "Well you're not having one."

Cassie explained that she and her colleague would be taking notes from which they would produce a summary of the meeting, but this would not be verbatim and would be sent to the Traders to be signed as agreed.

"We won't be signing it," Deputy Dawg barked.

Cassie continued unabated, "If the summary indicates that you said something that you didn't, then please put the amendment you believe is required on a separate sheet of paper."

"We won't be signing it," Deputy Dawg barked again.

Cassie continued, "If you don't return the summary of the noted meeting we shall regard it as agreed."

"It won't be agreed," Deputy Dawg was getting closer to a growl now.

"Without a copy of your recording or details of the amendments you believe are required, HMRC has nothing else to go on, other than the summary which we have already said would be regarded as agreed if no response is received." "If it's wrong, we will tell you," Deputy Dawg was beginning to get dog tired.

The meeting continued with less barking, until a point was reached when Deputy Dawg said, "Would you please leave the room I wish to speak to my client alone."

A few minutes later Deputy Dawg called the HMRC Officers back into the room and put forward his client's proposals as to how much his client was willing to pay. Cassie replied that this wasn't acceptable and made a counter proposal. After some horse trading, which didn't involve Deputy Dawg's horses that Cassie had fantasised had been tied up in the car park, they arrived at a figure which was acceptable to both sides. Shortly thereafter the meeting came to an end. As it was to turn out, this was roughly the figure of tax interest and penalties which would eventually be agreed and paid by the Trader but first, as they say, every dog has its day and Deputy Dawg wanted his. Having received the summary of the meeting, Deputy Dawg had emailed Cassie vehemently disagreeing with one sentence in HMRC's summary of the meeting. The sentence was insignificant and had no effect on the sum of the liability they had been discussing. Both Cassie and her colleagues' recollection and the contemporaneous handwritten notes supported the summary of the meeting. Cassie emailed Deputy Dawg advising him of this. In response Deputy Dawg emailed her a copy of his recording to prove that he was right and, indeed, he was. It was a small amendment to the summary that Cassie was happy to make. Deputy Dawg meanwhile, when he had provided Cassi with a copy of the recording of the meeting, something he had previously refused to do, had better still, provided a recording of the whole meeting, including the section when Cassie and her colleagues had stepped outside. In which she learned that the figure agreed was more than the Trader had wanted to pay and he thought that Cassie was a bitch. Very appropriate for Deputy Dawg's client. If Deputy Dawg had realised what he had done he might well have said, "Cotton picking muskrat".

When Wilfred Jennings had asked Cassie and her colleagues to leave the room he appeared to be feeling happy at the prospect of reducing Bill Michelin's tax bill. As he opened the door to invite the HMRC officers back in he appeared to be feeling grumpy. As Alan would say, two down five to go. After everyone had sat back down Jennings said dejectedly, "My client has nothing to add to his Outline Disclosure."

"Who was Mossi Moskovitch?" Cassie wondered. "Who could organise three masked men to threaten an old couple and turn a big jovial bloke like Michelin into a mute."

It was a rainy Thursday afternoon and Cassie had just finished her lunch break which she had spent in Cabot Circus seeking inspiration for a birthday present for Shaun and searching for a new everyday handbag for herself. She was unsuccessful on both scores. So, she was pleased to find emails in her inbox. The emails were from UK banks in response to the Financial Information Notices she had sent to the bank with whom Celtic Foods Ltd had an account, into which had been paid the £50,000 advance for the shareholders and the response from the Welsh bank used by the Welsh government to pay the £500,000 grant to Dragon Foods Ltd. The emails indicated that the £50,000 had been received from an account with the UK subsidiary of an online bank based in Sofia, called Bulgar-IT. The £500,000 had also been paid into an account with the same UK subsidiary of Bulgar-IT. The subsidiary of Bulgar-IT had gone into administration. The customers of the UK subsidiary of Bulgar-IT could lose their money and Bulgar-IT probably summed up their feelings. Cassie rang the administrators of Bulgar-IT UK, Coates & Perryman and established that they had electronic copies of the bank statements for all of the bank's customers covering the periods in which the £50,000 was paid and the £500,000 was received. Cassie got authorisation to issue Financial Information Notices to the administrators for the bank statements of the accounts into which the £500,000 had been paid and the account from which the £50,000 had been paid.

"The music has stopped and another layer of wrapping paper has come off, but no prize yet. How many more layers will there be?" Cassie thought.

CHAPTER TWELVE

It was a fresh morning and Cassie was just walking past the lifts when one opened and Alan walked out.

"I didn't think you were in today," Cassie said.

"Banksy has let me down, case of man-flu" Alan replied.

"Can't you play golf on your own?" Cassie enquired.

"Where's the fun in that, it's like drinking alone. By the way, I've got a new case for you which needs a woman's touch. I'll pop over later for a chat about it."

A little later Alan walked towards Cassie's desk and, spotting a free chair, wheeled it over and sat down. He was still making himself comfortable when Cassie said, "So, I need a box of tissues in my briefcase for this investigation?"

Alan laughed and replied, "I think there is a good chance you will. I know women crying gets you nowhere, not like what it means when a bloke cries."

"100% guilty," Cassie answered.

Alan's eyes glinted with delight at how well Cassie had absorbed what he had tried to teach her over the years. "There are worse fates than having the Trader crying. Did I ever tell you about my first investigative interview with a Trader?" Alan asked.

Cassie shook her head. Alan continued, "It was an enquiry meeting in the tax office. There was myself, a more experienced female colleague and the Trader, who was a female Tax Advisor so she had decided she didn't need professional representation. The purpose of the enquiry was checking whether all of the expenses she had claimed were allowable. She turned up for the meeting with a baby in a pram and when I started the meeting she took the baby from the pram and held it in her arms. I had just begun to ask her about the excessive expenses when she opened up her blouse and started breastfeeding. I didn't know where to look. Needless to say, my female colleague found the whole thing hilarious. As for me, like the baby, I felt a right tit."

"So, this new case?" Cassie enquired.

"Oh yes," Alan explained, "Big Tim, the manager on the CT Aspect Team, rang yesterday. One of the lads on his team had an interesting call from a woman regarding the director of the company they had opened an enquiry into. She mentioned tax fraud and that she had details of his Swiss bank account. Why don't you swing down to Big Tim's team and have a word."

Big Tim's team was a CT Aspect team which meant they would open enquiries into one or two aspects of a company's Corporation Tax (CT) return. For example, the expense of repairs in the accounts were almost double the expense claims for repairs in the previous year's accounts. The CT enquiry would be opened to check if some or all of these repair expenses were actually capital improvements to an asset.

Yes, CT aspect work really was as boring as it sounds. Cassie was glad she was on Alan's team and not on Big Tim's.

Cassie walked down the stairs to the second floor where she found Big Tim's team. Big Tim was big, 6'4", with fairly thin legs but a big beer gut. He was wearing trousers that he had bought online from America as it was difficult to get decent trousers in his own size in the UK. His shirt looked like maternity wear but it was ironed and the Bath Rugby Club tie completed his typical work attire. He had dark hair and a ruddy face. It was hard to tell how old he was, he could have been anything between 30 and 50. Big Tim smiled at Cassie and said, "Alan told me you were coming down, I'll take you over to Mike," Mike was the officer who had taken the phone call. There were about twenty-five people on Big Tim's team made up of new recruits and people who enjoyed doing CT aspect work. Mike was one such person. He was very good technically but didn't like the confrontation that could happen in a meeting so, as CT aspect work was almost entirely done by correspondence, it suited him. Mike was in his thirties and still lived at home with his Mum and Dad. He was wearing a brown suit and beige shirt that his Mum had ironed for him, completed with a purple tie that his Auntie had got him for Christmas. His hair had a number 1 cut as he was going thin on top, but the Grant Mitchell look didn't quite suit him as his neck and shoulders carried little to no muscle.

Mike explained that he had opened an enquiry into the Corporation Tax Return of a property investment company called EM Holdings Limited, the Sole Director of the company was Edward Mullery. Mike had received a call from Pippa Tait. She had explained that she had seen Mike's telephone number on a letter he had sent to Edward Mullery about EM Holdings Ltd when she had been visiting Mullery's house to collect their son, Sky. Pippa Tait had advised Mike that she had information on Mullery that would be of interest to HMRC and she had mentioned that she had details of his bank account. She had left her telephone number and address. Cassie copied down the information and thanked Mike for his time.

When Cassie got back, she told Alan what Mike had told her.

"A woman scorned is always a good source of Intel. You'd better go and see her."

Cassie rang Pippa Tait and arranged a mutually convenient date and time for her and Carl to visit. Cassie asked Pippa about the Swiss bank account details and Pippa told Cassie she would have these ready for when Cassie arrived.

The journey up to London was relatively pleasant, it was a sunny day and the traffic on the M25 had, at least, been moving. After finding somewhere to park, Cassie and Carl walked to Pippa Tait's flat. It was in a three-storey building. Pippa showed them through to a large kitchen-diner painted yellow, complete with the ubiquitous Aga and a large oak kitchen table. Cassie wondered if the Aga was there when they moved in or if they had had it installed after they had moved in complete with reinforced floor. Either way it had cost a lot of money Cassie thought, "And I would have chosen orange for my Aga, not that boring brown colour." Wearing head to toe Burberry, with expensive Knightsbridge shoes and balayage hair, Pippa offered them refreshments and then brought out a very inviting plate of biscuits. As they drank their tea and Carl helped himself to the biscuit he'd had his eye on, Pippa told her tale of woe. It had all seemed wonderful in the beginning. Edward Mullery, or the 'father of my child', as Pippa insisted on calling him, had seemed lovely, a true gentleman despite being somewhat older than herself. They had had a child together, Sky, but his father had been reluctant to marry Pippa, having already lost the majority of his fortune when his wife had divorced him. She had later died leaving his money, as he saw it, to his two grown up sons, who were now richer than him, thanks to his own money.

Life together had not been as Pippa had hoped. Whilst he had seemed debonair when he was taking her to expensive restaurants, he didn't seem so debonair when she was cleaning his shitty Y-fronts. Cleaning an old man's shitty Y-fronts was not how Pippa wanted to spend the rest of her life. "We clearly weren't compatible, but we had a child together. It was his responsibility to look after us, but what did he do? He bought this flat for us, in

Fulham." Pippa spat out the word Fulham with distaste. "It's miles away from my friends in Mayfair and Sky's little chums too."

On cue Cassie got the box of tissues out of her briefcase and placed them in front of Pippa who took one and blew her nose. Cassie took the opportunity, in a pause of Pippa's domestic dialogue, to change the subject from shitty Y-fronts to the reason for their visit. "You said you would have the Swiss bank account details for me."

"Of course," said Pippa and pulled a paper folder on the table towards her. She took out two pieces of paper and handed them to Cassie. Cassie glanced at the paper, it was very good quality writing paper. On the first sheet was the name and address of a bank in Switzerland and an account, name, sort code and account number. On the second sheet were the addresses of two properties, dates of sale, the names of the purchasers and two figures of purchase price.

Pippa explained that with each of these property sales Mullery had suggested to the purchaser that they declare the sales figure to be lower than the actual sales figure. He also suggested that the purchaser pay this difference into his Swiss bank account. The purchaser would save on the Stamp Duty Land Tax paid to the HMRC.

"Winner Winner Chicken Dinner," thought Cassie.

The first sale had been under-declared by £750,000, the second by £1 million. Cassie questioned Pippa further but she didn't know any additional details, nor did she have any useful documents or other information. Pippa continued her tale of woe, "The father of my child had promised when Sky was born that he would pay for Sky to go to Eton. Just as he and his two grown up sons had done. But he still hasn't arranged this and Sky is ten now."

Cassie thought to herself, "This woman is out for revenge but it hasn't occurred to her that, after I am finished with the father of her child, he may not have the money to send Sky to Eton even if he wanted to."

Pippa then said, "I have been seeing a therapist to get over the trauma of the break up. She suggested I write an on-line blog to help me recover."

"A blog!" Cassie thought, "how about a job instead."

"I've printed off a copy of my blog for you, you can take it away with you if you like," Pippa offered. Cassie looked at the pile of papers, imaginatively entitled "My Blog," which Pippa had pulled from the folder on the kitchen table and then Cassie looked down at her briefcase.

"The box of tissues will be staying in Fulham," Cassie thought.

Cassie thanked Pippa for the blog and advised her HMRC would not be able to provide her with any information regarding whatever action they would decide to take with the information that Pippa had given her. Nor did HMRC wish Pippa to take any action to obtain any further information. Carl managed to sneak another of the delicious biscuits in before Cassie stood to take her leave.

When Cassie got back to the office Alan was waiting ready to learn what she had found out.

"So, was she a woman scorned then?" Alan asked.

"Yes, but I wouldn't mind being as hard done by as she has been," Cassie replied.

Cassie then provided Alan with a description of the information she had obtained. Alan knew Cassie well and was fully aware of the answer to his question before he asked it. "You know what this means?"

"Spin offs," Cassie replied. Cassie loved a spin off. They had started with Edward Mullary, they now knew that he had deliberately under-declared the proceeds from the sale of his properties by £1,750,000 and also that two other Traders had committed tax fraud by deliberately under-declaring the Stamp Duty Land Tax in respect of the properties they had purchased from Edward Mullary.

Next day Cassie began to read through the blog, of which there were over 200 pages. Pippa clearly loved an acronym, the father of my child (TFOMC) Cassie got used to and shitty old man's Y-fronts (SOMY), but Cassie had to flick back quite a few pages to discover that (SAGP) was Sky's African Grey Parrot. There was absolutely nothing of interest to HMRC in the blog but Cassie had, of course, to read it all to discover this. There was one page of the blog which Cassie showed to Alan. Pippa had been crying into her Pimms, sitting on her own in what Cassie imagined to be a very expensive bar in Chelsea. When the well-known Chairman of a Premiership football team had sent one of his minders over with a drink for her.

"That doesn't happen in the Seven Stars," Alan commented.

Criminal Investigations had declined all three cases and Cassie had been given these cases to review.

Cassie began by reviewing Edward Mullary's tax affairs. It didn't take her long to work out what he did to make money. He would purchase the leasehold interest of an expensive London property with a relatively short lease. He would then seek to extend or obtain a new longer lease from the freeholder taking the freeholder to court if necessary. Having obtained the longer lease he would then sell the lease at a sizable profit. Cassie couldn't find any other potential tax frauds connected to Mullary beyond the £1,750,000 identified by Pippa.

Cassie next reviewed George Buckle who had under-declared the purchase price of the property he had bought from Mullary by £1 million. Cassie identified that Buckle had a number of other properties, two of which he had sold without declaring the Capital Gains he had made on the sale of the properties.

Lastly, she had reviewed Sebastian Clemence. In addition to the Stamp Duty Land Tax fraud,

Clemence had almost a street of properties in Cheltenham which he had inherited four years ago but had yet to declare any rental income from. Cassie's research indicated that all of these properties were occupied and therefore most likely paying rent to Sebastian Clemence which he was not declaring.

Cassie completed her reviews and submitted them to Alan for authorisation, which he gave.

Cassie wrote to each of the Traders advising them that HMRC had reason to suspect them of tax fraud and they were being investigated under Code of Practice 9. All three Traders accepted the offer and made Outline Disclosures which included all of the tax frauds which Cassie had identified in her review.

The first meeting to be arranged was with Mullary. The meeting took place at HMRC's offices in Bristol, so no fancy biscuits this time, just a jug of water and some paper cups. Mullary had selected one of the big firms to represent him. Things ran smoothly there were, after all, only two transactions to look at, but Cassie would want bank statements for the Swiss bank account for the past six years. She would also suggest that the tax advisors analyse these in Mullary's Disclosure Report, identifying all bankings and payments made out of the account.

Mullary confirmed that there were only two tax frauds and Cassie explained to him that he would be asked to sign a Certificate of Full Disclosure and, if it was later found out that he had committed other tax frauds, he could be criminally investigated with a view to a prosecution. The start of the meeting wasn't that interesting. What was interesting, or at least of note, was Mullary himself. The first thought that went through Cassie's mind when she met him was Mrs Murton's question to Debbie McGee, "What first attracted you to the millionaire Paul Daniels?"

He looked every one of the thirty years he was older than Pippa. He was dressed in a tweed jacket, checked shirt and tie and the salmon pink trousers that men of a certain age think look good. The tweed jacket had been top quality when new, it now looked tatty. Which wasn't helped by some very obvious repairs.

The obvious repairs made Cassie think of her Gran. Her Gran had been a milliner by trade and she had been well known in the family for her invisible mending. The boyfriend of one of Cassie's cousins had been in a panic. He was in the Welsh Guards and somehow managed to get a hole in his ceremonial red uniform. Gran came to the rescue with her invisible mending, not only was the hole gone, but you couldn't see where it had been.

"A Regimental Sergeant Major inspecting you before Trooping the Colour wouldn't spot my invisible mending," Cassie's Gran had proudly claimed.

Cassie looked at Edward Mullary and thought, "There was no such fine repair work on his tweed jacket. And was that egg on his tie? How could this man ever have been thought to be debonair? I had a Saga lout try to chat me up when Shaun and I were on holiday, despite the fact that he was old enough to have been my Grandad, but at least he had some get up and go. If the man in front of me ever had any get up and go, it had got up and gone."

Mullary had a strange way of describing himself in the third person. So instead of saying I did this or I did that, he said Mullary did this or Mullary did that. The question that kept coming into Cassie's mind was, "Did Mullary have shitty Y-fronts under his salmon pink trousers?"

Cassie asked if Mullary would commission a Disclosure Report. Thankfully he replied "Yes" as, had he replied "Mullary does", Cassie would have then had to confirm if he had meant himself as she wouldn't want to face the possibility at some later date of, "My client was referring to his dog Mullary."

HMRC hadn't done so well with the last case with a defence of, "It's not me, it's my dog".

Mullary had agreed to prepare a Disclosure Report which was submitted three months later. Cassie understood from Mullary's tax advisors that he had to sell a studio flat to pay HMRC. This was, however, in Mayfair and sold for £1.2 million. Cassie was happy that this case had closed quickly. Pippa might also be happy if she ever found out what she had cost the 'father of my child'. The child himself? What did life have in store for him then? Cassie thought to herself, "He would probably go to the local Comp, change his name by Deed Poll and, unlike Mum and Dad, get a job."

The second meeting was with George Buckle. His Tax Advisors called themselves TAX - The Professionals. Cassie was unfamiliar with the firm so, as she always did under such circumstances, she googled them. From their website they clearly wished to project themselves as major players in the world of tax advisors dealing with Code of Practice 9 investigations. TAX - The Professionals saw themselves as a big fish in a small pond. In addition to the website there were also YouTube videos on Code of Practice 9 made by TAX - The Professionals.

The day of the meeting came and Cassie and Carl arrived at the offices of TAX - The Professionals. There was no reception, you stepped through the doorway into the main office into which three staff were crammed. After Cassie had introduced herself one of the staff offered them a coffee and returned with plastic cups. Cassie took a sip, it was disgusting. Cassie had visited Traders, including a garage where you could see the oil floating on top of the coffee. This tasted worse. There was nowhere to put it down. Carl was ahead of the game engaging one of the staff in conversation, approaching her desk seemingly to hear her better, but leaving his cup on her desk. A young man then entered the office from the rear of the building and invited them into the board room. Cassie and Carl were the first people into what was laughably called a Board Room. They squeezed their way between the glass table and the wall.

"Big Fish in a Small Pond". Cassie was reminded of the interview stage of The Apprentice when one of the candidates claimed to be, "A Big Fish in a Small Pond". To which Claude Litner had replied, "Fish? You're not even a fish."

Cassie sat down, finding the leg room available to be so limited as to make the stalls in the Bristol Hippodrome feel like British Airways Club Class. No sooner had she sat down than the Trader, George

Buckle, entered with two Tax Advisors. The younger one who had shown them to the board room and an older Tax Advisor, who Cassie recognised from the YouTube videos. Buckle was wearing a suit in the manner of a man not accustomed to wearing one. He was stocky, but not fat, with a British Bulldog face, but it was the large amethyst ring that got Cassie's attention. She knew amethyst was not in the Premier League of jewels, but one that size must be worth a few quid.

The meeting progressed as normal, Buckle admitting to the tax frauds on his Outline Disclosure. He also provided some further detail on the properties he had sold without declaring Capital Gains. It was only when Cassie got off the subject of the frauds covered by the Outline Disclosure that the older Tax Advisor got a bit aggressive. Cassie asked Buckle about a dissolved company of which he had been a director and produced a Profit and Loss account which showed £30,000 wages had been paid. The older Tax Advisor shouted at Cassie, "You are breaking GDPR rules by providing that data to my client."

Cassie was somewhat taken aback, she didn't want to get into a long debate about this, so she replied, "The company no longer exists as a person in law," and turning to Buckle she asked, "Who were the £30,000 wages paid to?"

"Agnes", Buckle replied.

"Who is she?" Cassie asked.

"My ex-girlfriend from Poland," Buckle mumbled.

"Did the company operate Pay-As-You-Earn against the wages?" Cassie asked. Buckle didn't reply so Cassie replied for him, "No, it didn't, as the company had no Pay-As-You-Earn scheme". "What is Agnes' surname?" Cassie continued.

Buckle replied, "Rasiak".

"What did Agnes do to earn this £30,000?" Cassie queried.

"She answered the phone," Buckle responded.

"Was this £30,000 paid into her bank account or yours?" Cassie continued relentlessly.

"I don't remember," answered Buckle, returning to a mumble.

"Perhaps we should contact Agnes and ask her?" Cassie suggested.

"No, it was my account," Buckle replied desperately.

"He really doesn't want me to talk to Agnes," Cassie thought. "I wonder why, I guess we will never know, it's highly unlikely we could ever trace her but I thought a bluff might work."

"Why didn't you declare this £30,000 payment before?" Cassie asked.

"I don't remember," said Buckle.

"Which bank account was the £30,000 paid into? We will want to see the statements for this account to check what else was paid into it. Is there anything else you wish to tell me?" Cassie asked.

Buckle replied, "Yes," then paused before stating that his current girlfriend was receiving a wage from his latest company which was also paid into his bank account.

Cassie explained that, as this was not included in Buckle's Outline Disclosure, it was not covered by the agreement that HMRC would not investigate the fraud with a view to a criminal prosecution. She suggested that now might be a good time for a comfort break. Cassie asked which way to the toilet. She found it but, on her way back to the board room, she must have taken a wrong turn and she found herself behind the counter of the coffee shop next door to TAX - The Professionals. She spun on her heel and headed back to the Tax Advisors' office. Seconds later she realised she had missed a trick as she felt certain that Alan, in the same position, would have shouted something like, "Large latte for Mike," before disappearing. Perhaps she wasn't ready to fill his shoes just yet.

On her way back from the toilets to the board room she met Carl and suggested they leave the Tax Advisors' offices and step out into the street, telling the office staff on the way that they would be back. Once outside the office Cassie rang first Alan and then the manager of the Criminal Team. The advice was to continue the investigation civilly. Having finished the telephone calls, Cassie told Carl about her impromptu coffee shop break.

Carl replied, "That's nothing. Do you remember the bloke we had who thought a comfort break in the meeting was a cocaine break?"

Cassie smiled and said, "Let's get back in."

After they returned to the meeting Buckle agreed to commission a Disclosure Report to be completed in six months by TAX - The Professionals. Twelve months later this was submitted to HMRC. Cassie checked the Disclosure Report. TAX - The Professionals' calculations were generously in their client's favour. It took another two months of emails back and forth before the figures were agreed of the tax due that were acceptable to Cassie. Next to be agreed were the penalties authorised by Alan and lastly the interest.

The investigation was settled by a Contract Settlement. A Contract Settlement is where both sides have agreed the sum of Tax Penalties and interest due. The Trader then offers to pay the sum, usually within thirty days. HMRC issues a letter accepting the offer and the Trader then makes payment of the sum. No assessments, all very straightforward. Due to EU law, however, you can't do a contract settlement for VAT.

During the Brexit campaign Alan's team, like most of the country, was split pretty evenly between Brexiteers and Remainers but, when the result was announced, the team were united in the thought, "Great, we can do Contract Settlements for VAT now."

All these years later we are still waiting. Which is either proof we should have never left, or yet another missed opportunity to benefit from Brexit, depending on your point of view.

Sebastian Clemence, who had fraudulently under-declared the purchase of a property by £750,000 to evade paying the full amount of Stamp Duty Land Tax due, was originally from Newcastle, but now lived in Spain. He had asked that the opening meeting with HMRC take place in Newcastle. Cassie and Carl had flown up the night before the meeting and, by some miracle, HMRC had booked a flight that arrived by 1800 and not after midnight, as per usual.

Cassie and Carl arrived at their hotel by taxi from the airport. Only to be told by reception that the hotel had double booked their rooms and the taxi had been booked to take them to another hotel. As they waited for the taxi Cassie wished they had asked the first taxi to wait for them. After about ten minutes the free taxi arrived and it was only a short distance to the replacement hotel. As they entered the reception lobby it was clear that there was some big do on, to which they were not invited. They agreed to dump their bags in their rooms and go straight out. Half an hour later Cassie was sitting outside a cafe bar by the river. Admiring the bridges for which Newcastle is famous, she sipped at the large glass of Sauvignon Blanc in one hand, as she popped a very juicy stuffed olive into her mouth with the other. Carl meanwhile, was standing a little away from Cassie on the phone to his wife. He didn't appear to be doing much talking but instead was nodding and drinking his lager. Shaun always said he drank faster standing up and the speed Carl's glass was emptying backed this up Cassie thought to herself. On the subject of Shaun, she would ring him later, right now she was enjoying the view, the wine and the olives.

The next morning felt like quite a lazy one. Cassie had decided to give her morning run a miss and instead of her usual morning rush she could take her time. She put on the breakfast news and made herself a cup of tea. She looked around the room, everything was new, albeit the fact that the milk was long life milk. She had felt so tired last night she hadn't really noticed how new the room looked. She finished her tea and then had a shower and began to get ready. As she put on her make-up it occurred to her the TV sounded louder in the bathroom than in the bedroom. Closing the bathroom door, she confirmed that she was right, the TV was being piped into a speaker in the bathroom. "Whatever next". It made her think of home when Barney would have his music going in the bathroom as he had a shower.

Cassie had agreed to meet Carl for breakfast at 8.30 am. Carl had arrived early and when she joined him, he informed her, "There was a big slap-up meal here last night. It was the grand opening of the hotel and the food was prepared by Marco Pierre White and, better still, he is doing the breakfast this morning as well."

Cassie didn't normally have a cooked breakfast when staying in a hotel but today she would make an exception. They placed their orders and a little while later their breakfasts arrived. Carl dived straight in while Cassie sipped her second cup of tea this morning. This one tasted all the better for it being fresh milk. She then tried a piece of the sausage. She had to admit, as she finished her breakfast, that this was the best hotel breakfast she had ever had and the sausage was to die for. Carl beckoned over the waitress to ask for another sausage.

"Only one sausage per customer," she replied.

Carl smiled and then winked at her and said, "Go on".

Five minutes later Carl had a second sausage.

At 10.25 am Cassie and Carl arrived at the offices of the tax advisors Carter-Vickers.
The offices had been built twenty years ago but more recently refurbished, furnished with glass and stainless steel, looking very smart and up-to-date. Everything was very professional.

Clemence was slim, tall with dark hair and in his forties. He was smartly dressed and his tanned skin indicated he didn't live in Newcastle. They were shown into the meeting room which could have seated twenty with ease, unlike their last meeting. In the meeting room the Trader and the two Tax Advisors were waiting. Cassie shook hands with each of them. Before the meeting began the Tax Advisors from Carter-Vickers handed Cassie what they called an expansion on the Outline Disclosure. Cassie flipped quickly through it. This document contained a lot more detail than many a Disclosure Report she had been handed after six months of so-called work by the tax advisors.

Five minutes or so after Cassie began the meeting Clemence started crying. She hadn't even asked him a question yet. His crying continued, through which he kept babbling on about how he couldn't believe that his wife had left him and the kids, for that short, balding, fat, ginger, incredibly boring bloke, Neville, that they had met at the golf club.

The Tax Advisors suggested that they recommence after a thirty-minute break. Cassie and Carl left Carter-Vickers' office and found a small Italian cafe where they ordered two coffees. They sat there for a while without saying anything before Carl said, "Neville is either loaded, or he has to tuck it in his sock."
Cassie laughed. After finishing their coffees they returned to the offices of Carter-Vickers. Once back in the meeting room they were joined by Clemence and his Tax Advisors. Cassie had barely started when Clemence was crying again.

"Don't cry for me Marbella," Cassie thought.

Cassie put her interview brief to one side and asked Clemence if he would commission a Disclosure Report. Which he said he would. She then asked who did he want to prepare it. To which he replied simply, "Them". With that his crying got louder and his body began to shake. The junior of the two Tax Advisors escorted him from the room. Cassie arranged with the older Tax Advisor that she would ring him the following afternoon to discuss the contents of the Disclosure Report, once she had a chance to read through the work they had already done.

The next day after reviewing the work already done Cassie was satisfied with it and was happy that there wouldn't be a lot of work required to turn this into a Disclosure Report.

A couple of months later Cassie settled her investigation into Sebastian Clemence. The two spin off investigations had between them over £250,000 in extra tax, interest and penalties paid to HMRC.

"Better than a poke in the eye with a sharp stick as Dad would say," thought Cassie. Before imagining the horror in a primary school nowadays if a toddler told the teacher, "My Daddy says that's better than a poke in the eye with a sharp stick."

CHAPTER THIRTEEN

It was Thursday lunch-time and Cassie had just eaten the buckwheat salad that she had made last night. She decided it was time to do some work so she closed down the online news site that she had been looking at. She had found it hard anyway to find any news on this news site.

"Celebrity on beach in bikini," if a celebrity hadn't been wearing a bikini to the beach that might have been a story.

"Celebrity breaks cover," or, in other words, the celebrity who we wrote a story about yesterday goes to the corner shop and buys some milk.

"Police quiz murder suspect."

Police: "What do surgeons wear in the operating theatre?"

Suspect: "Scrubs"

Police: "Correct, one point, and that's also where you'll be going."

Having logged onto her work terminal Cassie checked her email inbox. There was an email from the administrators of Bulgar-IT Limited. Cassie hoped that the bank statements attached to the email would show into which bank account the £500,000 had been paid by the Welsh government and/or from which bank account the £50,000 had been paid to the shareholders of Celtic Foods Limited. As she looked at the statement her forehead wrinkled into a frown. The bank account used for these transactions belonged to a company called Green Turtle. The administrators did not hold any bank account details for the account in the name of Green Turtle Limited. Per Companies House's records Green Turtle Limited had been in existence for three months. The company had not registered with HMRC as being liable for VAT nor as an employer operating Pay-As-You-Earn. Companies House's records showed the director and shareholder was a Chinese man born in May 2000 called Mr I Qu. The registered office of the company, which was also given as the director's contact address, was an address Cassie knew well. It was an address in London given by thousands of companies. What was known as a 'Brass Plate address'.

"The saying goes, 'Where there's muck there's brass', but with this address, where there's brass there's muck and very difficult to trace," thought Cassie. "Well, there's always Google."

From a search of the internet Cassie discovered that Green Turtle Limited was a very short-lived Crypto currency trading website. Cassie was, therefore, unable to find the next account to follow the money, so her process of unwrapping the present had come to an end as the information she required was stuck on a block chain somewhere in the world.

Cassie tried to cheer herself up with the thought, "the crime will out". Which made her recollect another of her Dad's Royal Navy stories. His story was that he was skiing with the Royal Navy. Why would the Royal Navy need to be skiing? Sometimes she thought that her Dad's stories were as likely to be true as Uncle Albert's 'during the war' tales. Anyway, Cassie's Dad had been one of six young sailors skiing with an officer and a Chief Petty Officer. They had stopped for a hot chocolate and, when they had started off again, her Dad had realised that someone had nicked one of his ski poles. Her Dad informed the Chief Petty Officer, who informed the officer.

The officer skied over to Cassie's Dad and said to him, "Well Holmes, when we stop for lunch there will be lots of people there, so do the good British thing and steal someone else's pole."

"Aye Aye Sir," Cassie's Dad had replied and after lunch he was the proud owner of two ski poles again.

The Chief Petty Officer then skied up to him and said, "Holmes, Sir wants his pole back".

Following the attack on the Liquidator and his resulting retirement, Cassie had appointed a new Liquidator who had, in turn, appointed a specialist firm of solicitors. This firm would be investigating the sale of the land by Wheat Ear Limited at millions of pounds under its true value. Coates Chambers, a top firm of London property lawyers, were now acting for Redland Farms Limited and were disputing the VOA's valuation of the land. They were proposing that the matter be listed for a hearing by a judge at a tribunal to decide on the value of the land. Cassie knew that this might take years before any decision would be reached. What intrigued her was who actually had instructed and paid Coates Chambers. It was highly unlikely to have been Sandy Williams, who appeared to have gone missing. The letters sent by HMRC to Sandy Williams' last known address had been returned with 'No Longer at This Address' written on them.

News from over the pond was somewhat better, Cassie's report had clearly sold the case to the IRS and they now wanted to have a video call. The purpose of which was to discuss Cassie's suggestion of a simultaneous inquiry into Yeheuda Rosenthal's tax affairs.

Sarah Rosenthal stirred the broth on the kitchen stove. There was not a lot of meat left on the bones that she was boiling up but she had vegetables that she had bought cheaply to boost the meal. She had bought them as she usually did just before the shop had thrown them away. This meal was for her, her husband Yeheudah and their six children. Plus, of course, the baby she was expecting. She and Yeheudah loved each other dearly, she loved Yeheudah for being such an honest, pious and hardworking man. He spent such long hours repairing shoes. They had discussed employing someone to help him in the business and of moving to a larger apartment but there was never enough money for them to save any money towards such luxuries. So, they continued to rent the small apartment. It had two bedrooms but they used three of the rooms as bedrooms and so the kitchen table became their living room. So, Sarah and Yeheudah's life continued, poor but happy. One day much the same as the next, but all that was to change.

A few weeks had passed since Cassie had learned of the IRS's interest in a simultaneous inquiry and today was the day for the video call with them. The meeting was arranged for 1530, to accommodate the difference in time zones. Cassie had decided to wear a smart white blouse and she noticed that Alan was wearing a shirt and tie. Alan and Cassie had a quick chat, but there wasn't much to discuss, either the IRS would go for the simultaneous enquiry idea or they wouldn't.

At 1525 Cassie and Alan joined the video call. Initially it was just themselves and then they were joined by Glyn, the officer from the Exchange of Information Team.

Five minutes later, bang on time, the IRS investigator Leroy and his manager Brad joined the video call, but Glyn's opposite number was still missing. Whilst Cassie and Alan and their American counterparts were keen to get started, Glyn didn't wish to break any protocols by proceeding without the US Gateway official, as he described her. For the next ten minutes they discussed the weather in their respective countries and Brad's trip to London. Brad apparently had been surprised that Spotted

Dick was a real dessert and not something invented by Harry Potter author JK Rowling.

Whitney, Glyn's opposite number, then joined the call with apologies for the IT issues that she had suffered. So, with both Gateways in place, the meeting could proceed. Brad advised that the IRS had decided to agree to the proposal of a simultaneous inquiry into Yeheudah Rosenthal's tax affairs. It was agreed by the parties on the call that the investigations would commence on Monday and a further video call was arranged to take place in six weeks' time when they would compare the responses received. In the end the chat about Brad's trip to London took longer than the actual business part of the video call. Cassie and Alan had what they wanted, a simultaneous enquiry. Cassie would have done pretty much anything to have achieved that, including eating Spotted Dick with school lumpy pink custard.

Cassie and Alan, after a long discussion, had decided they didn't want to write to Yeheudah under the Code of Practice 9, advising him that HMRC had reason to suspect him of tax fraud. This was because, whilst there was reason to suspect tax fraud, they both thought Mossi was behind it. Therefore, they decided the investigation would be worked as a Code of Practice 8. Cassie began her investigation by opening corporation tax enquiries into the tax returns made by the UK companies of which Yeheudah was shown by Companies House' records to be a director. Cassie also sent a covering letter to both Yeheudah's address in the UK as well as to Nigel Greenfield's address, which was shown as Yeheudah's address in the UK. In this covering letter Cassie set out in detail HMRC's queries as to his country of residence and where he got the money from to buy the properties in London. In total the letter ran to 23 pages.

That same Monday the IRS had written to Yeheudah asking that he ring them to discuss his tax affairs. Yeheudah thought little of the IRS's letter when he received it, putting it on the kitchen table unopened along with the other post to be dealt with, which were usually unpaid bills. It wasn't until he received and read Cassie's letter that he became worried, opened the IRS's letter as well and contacted his accountant, Joe Goldsmith. When Yeheudah contacted Joe Goldsmith it came as a bit of a shock to Joe, Yeheudah was the last client he would expect the IRS to investigate. When they met, Yeheudah handed Cassie's letter across the desk to Joe. Joe read it in silence, the repeated raising of his eyebrows indicated his surprise at its contents. Eventually he placed it on his desk, looked up at Yeheudah and asked, "Is it true, do you have properties in London, and if you do, why on earth didn't you tell me about them?"

"No, I don't," Yeheudah replied. "But my cousin in England did ask me to sign some documents. What does it all mean?" Yeheudah asked.

"Well, look at it from the IRS's perspective," Joe explained. "Your tax returns declare that you don't have two cents to rub together, yet you have millions of dollars of property offshore in London like some Rusky gangster."

"But I just have a very small shoe repair business," Yeheudah explained.
"Exactly," Joe replied, "the IRS and the Feds will figure that's just a front for your real business of drug dealing or some other illegal racket."

"How bad can this get?" Yeheudah asked.

"I'm not an expert, but you could end up serving time in the Pen," Joe explained before asking, "why did you sign these damn papers anyway?"

"You don't mess with my cousin," Yeheudah replied in a cowed voice as if somehow Mossi could be listening.

Joe tried to sound reassuring as he advised, "I'll give the IRS a ring and try to explain your position."

Later in the day Joe Goldsmith rang Leroy the IRS investigator to explain Yeheudah did not own any property inside the US or overseas. He had, however, signed some documents for a family member and this was how the confusion had arisen. Leroy had asked about Yeheudah's directorship of a number of offshore companies. Joe replied that his understanding was that this was all connected to the documents his client had signed and he stated that his client's only business interest was as a repairer of shoes.

Cassie's letter to Yeheudah may have crossed the Atlantic but it had still not been brought to the attention of Nigel Greenfield. Greenfield was in his early fifties. He was short and slim with thinning sandy coloured hair. At Greenfield & Co HMRC post was not given a high priority and, when the staff did get around to opening it, the letter was either scanned and emailed to Greenfield or put in a very large pile to be scanned and filed. When Greenfield did read Cassie's letter, he got up from his desk and took a key from his trouser pocket to open a locked electrical cabinet on the wall of the room in his home which he used as an office. Inside the cabinet was an array of Pay-As-You-Go mobile phones, of the brick variety, each with a charging cable feeding into a multiple power socket within the cabinet. Greenfield picked up the one that was labelled Mossi and rang the stored number. Mossi was forever changing his number for general use but for calls from Greenfield, the Solomons and Sandy Williams, he carried a separate phone.

"Mossi, I've had a letter from HMRC's fraud team addressed to Yeheudah saying that they are investigating him," Greenfield explained.

"So, what are you going to do about it?" Mossi asked.

"Mossi is blaming me this isn't good," thought Greenfield before replying, "We," he didn't say you, "don't need to do anything yet, but I will give Percival Parrott a ring to see what he advises."

Percival Parrott was 6'2", with dark hair and about 18 stone so that his belly bulged over the belt of his shorts. He enjoyed his morning strolls along the beach in Eilat, the water of the Red Sea was so clear you could wade into the sea and watch the small fish swim between your toes. He didn't want to get his feet wet just yet, that could wait until later in the privacy of his own pool. By the time he got back from his walk, Parrott was beginning to get a bit hot and sweaty and he was already looking forward to a Long Island iced tea beside his pool. It could get hot in Israel, even at this time of the year. Ten minutes later with his shirt off and the cold glass in his hand Parrott thought to himself, "Twenty replies to HMRC letters and then a couple of lengths of the pool."

A tax advisor responding to twenty HMRC letters you would think would take some considerable time, but not for Parrott. With the cocktail in one hand, he typed with his thumb on the mobile in his other hand, responding to HMRC's letters:

1. "We appeal everything."
2. "We want to review."
3. "That's rubbish."

There were seventeen letters left to reply to when Parrott's phone indicated that there was a call being received and it was Greenfield who was calling. It was annoying to be interrupted and having his swim delayed, but this was work and work paid for a life that he enjoyed. So, he answered with more bonhomie than he was feeling. Greenfield summarised the situation and sent a copy of Cassie's letter by email to Parrott's phone. Parrott looked at the top of Cassie's letter for the telephone number to ring and, without bothering to read the letter, rang Cassie.

Cassie picked up the phone, "Cassie Holmes-Smith, HMRC Fraud," she said.

"Percival Parrott here," came the reply, "I'm phoning about Yeheudah Rosenthal." Cassie made no reply. "This is a COP 8 I understand?" Again, Cassie made no reply. "One of the Board of HMRC was asking my advice only last week about COP 8 and COP 9 and whether they were fit for purpose." Parrott paused for Cassie to comment and, hearing no response, he continued, "It was after I had just won my latest appeal at the first tier tax tribunal, perhaps you read it?" Parrott didn't expect Cassie to reply to be honest, he hadn't even read the whole of the judgement himself, so he continued. "Anyway, Yeheudah Rosenthal, it all seems to have been some big mistake. Of course, he has no money and, between you and me, I don't think he's that bright. So, you might as well close down your investigation."

Cassie now spoke. "I have no written authority for you to act on Yeheudah Rosenthal's behalf."

"I can get that," Parrott replied.

"I look forward to speaking with you when you do," Cassie said, seconds before putting the phone down. Cassie smiled and wondered what Parrott's next move would be. Talk to one of the 'Board' perhaps? Likely story.

"Harrumph," was the sound that came out of Parrott's mouth. Putting down his phone and his cocktail, he stripped to his trunks and went for a swim.

Parrott's arrogance didn't phase Cassie and neither would his talent as a swimmer if she could only see him splashing around now.

One look at Cassie's shapely, toned shoulders told anyone admiring this beautiful woman that she had once been a swimmer. Not only a swimmer but a competitive synchronised swimmer, now commonly known as Artistic Swimming.

Shaun had arranged for him and his father to pick her up from training to go on to their first date while they were still teenagers at school. Instead of being dressed to impress, Cassie was stomping down the pavement towards the car, in tears, with bare feet, head down and dripping wet, still in her swimsuit. Shaun watched, his mouth hanging open as she flung herself into the back of the car. Neither he nor his father knew what to say. Between her sobs, she managed to tell them that someone had stolen her clothes, shoes, towels, hairbrush and bag. What a first date that turned out to be. All these years later, she could look back and laugh about it and had forgiven Shaun's dad for shamelessly laughing out loud as he had driven her home to get dressed.

Nigel Greenfield posted the responses to the Corporation Tax enquiries that Cassie had opened into the Corporation Tax Returns, submitted by the companies of which Yeheudah Rosenthal was a director. He placed Cassie's covering letter on his to-do pile.

Over thirty days had passed since Cassie had opened her Code of Practice 8 investigation into Yeheudah's tax affairs. Greenfield's responses to the eight Enquiry Notices were almost identical for each of the companies. It was stated that a property was held by Yeheudah in trust for the company and the legal document was provided to demonstrate this, signed by Yeheudah Rosenthal. What wasn't provided were the company's bank statements, the mortgage applications or the statements of payment.

Cassie laughed out loud, her colleagues looked at her in surprise and Alan got up from his seat and came over to her desk, in order to discover the source of Cassie's amusement. Cassie looked up when Alan's shadow moved across her desk.

"What's tickled you then?" Alan asked.

"Mossi's residence is, according to the trust documents, held in trust by Yeheudah Rosenthal for MM Properties Limited. MM or Mossi Moscovitch, not YR for Yeheudah Rossenthal," Cassie replied.

"Cheeky bugger," Alan laughed.

Cassie was, therefore, today issuing formal Information Notices to Yeheudah Rosenthal and the eight companies of which he was a director, requiring the production of the documents and the information she needed for her investigation.

She posted the Information Notices in respect of Yeheudah Rosenthal to his New York address and to Nigel Greenfield. The other information notices to the companies were sent to the contact address which was Nigel Greenfield's office. Cassie also emailed Nigel Greenfield advising him that if he wished to correspond with her by email she would need his client's written consent that she might do so. Nigel Greenfield read Cassie's email. "It would make things easier," he thought, "but it also meant speaking to Mossi to get Yeheudah Rosenthal's email address." With some temerity he unlocked the electrical cabinet and retrieved the phone. Fortunately, Mossi seemed to be in a good mood, he provided Nigel Greenfield with his cousin's mobile number and work email address. He laughed as he explained that his cousin wouldn't have an iphone as it was a gateway to evil.

"Evil?" queried Nigel Greenfield.

"Sex," Mossi replied, still laughing and then hung up.

Nigel Greenfield had emailed Yeheudah the email consent forms to be signed and returned. However, two days later, having not received them, he rang Yeheudah. He began by explaining to Yeheudah that there was an HMRC check going on, but it was nothing to worry about. He was taken aback to learn from Yeheudah that the IRS were also investigating.

"What have you told them?" he asked.

"My Tax Attorney has told the IRS that they have nothing to do with me," Yeheudah replied.

"You can't do that," Greenfield exclaimed in shock as the consequences for himself of angering Mossi went through his mind.

Quite reasonably Yeheudah replied, "Why not?"

Greenfield began to try to explain that per Land Registry records the properties were registered in Yeheudah's name, but he gave up when Yeheudah replied, "But they are not mine." So, he tried another tack, "Can you sign and return to me those consent forms."

"I have a PC and printer/scanner at the shop," Yeheudah advised, "I will sign those forms and email you the signed copies."

Nigel Greenfield was grateful for this small step forward and, after obtaining Joe Goldsmith's details from Yeheudah, he tried to convince him that everything would be okay in the end, but for now Yeheudah must say his advisors were looking into it.

"But why?" Yeheudah cried.

"Because, per the legal documentation, you own them and for now you need to stall, or tell Mossi why," Nigel Greenfield explained. Yeheudah duly rang Joe Goldsmith to explain that things were more complex than he thought and needed to be looked into. Joe Goldsmith reluctantly had related this new explanation to Leroy at the IRS.

The second video conference call with the IRS was much more relaxed than the first and, after a few minutes of preliminaries, it became a conversation between investigators.

"We have had very little from the company's Tax Advisors and nothing at all from Yeheudah or his Tax Advisors. His Tax Advisor and the company's Tax Advisor, being one and the same, Nigel Greenfield," Cassie explained.

"We got a call from Yeheudah's Tax Attorney in which he stated the properties were nothing to do with his client," Leroy advised. Cassie and Alan looked at each other and smiled, but Leroy continued, "He then rang again a few days later stating that the ownership of the properties was more complex than his client had first thought and they would need to do some further work to establish the facts."

"So, what will you do next then?" Cassie enquired.

"We will ask for a video call with Yeheudah and his Tax Attorney and, if that's a no show, we will summons him," Leroy replied. The US Exchange of Information Officer was shifting nervously in her seat at this free exchange of information.

"What would you guys do next?" Leroy asked. This time it was HMRC's Exchange of Information Officer who was moving first this way and then that, like someone with ants in their pants.

"As the companies have not complied with the Information Notices, we will issue penalties and then we will use Financial Information Notices to go to the companies' banks and the financial institutions who lent the money to Yeheudah to purchase the properties," Cassie responded.

"We sure would like to see any loan applications," Leroy commented. "Yeah," said Brad in approval.

There was a certain amount of huffing and puffing from HMRC's Exchange of Information Officer before Alan concluded the discussion by suggesting they reconvene in six weeks' time to compare notes again.

Later that evening Cassie and Sean were enjoying a date night. They hadn't gone anywhere because they didn't quite trust the kids to be in the house on their own for too long, despite being older teenagers or, as they liked to call themselves, young adults. But they had agreed to make themselves scarce. Barney was in his room with his headphones on playing on his play station trying not to think of Mum and Dad being romantic. Every time he thought about him and his sister, he realised that his parents had had sex at least twice, and that was twice too many times in his opinion. And Wendy was texting her friends organising their lives as well as her own. It didn't matter what they did as long as they stayed out of trouble, Cassie was enjoying some grown up time with her childhood sweetheart. With the meal finished they sipped their wine and Cassie excitedly told Sean about her latest investigation. She explained that she had issued penalties to the companies she was investigating for not having complied with the Information Notices. Sean then asked, "So what?" Cassie explained that the lack of compliance with the notices now meant she could use another HMRC power to go directly to the banks for the mortgage applications and bank statements which she wanted. Sean asked, "Why do you have to jump through so many hoops to do your job?" Cassie replied, "Because that's the law." Sean then said, "I don't know how you have the patience to do it. It seems to me that the law protects the tax fraudsters rather than aiding the investigators."

A few days later she had a response from a financial institution. It took only two weeks for the financial institution who had lent the money to purchase five of the properties to provide the mortgage applications and payment statement. Cassie then passed these mortgage applications to the Exchange of Information team, in order that they could be emailed to the IRS prior to their next video call.
It was the day of the third video call with the IRS, things were beginning to get even more relaxed. Cassie had worn an every-day work blouse instead of dressing for a meeting and Alan had decided not to cancel a lunchtime drink with some old colleagues and instead decided to leave the get-together to return to the office for the video call.

As Alan took a last gulp of his Old Speckled Hen he looked around at his retired former colleagues sitting at the pub table in the Shakespeare and he said, "Mel Gibson, Sly Stallone and Arnie had sat in a big movie producer's office. As a young movie executive pitches an idea for a movie about the classical composers Mel can't decide if he's Brahms or Liszt and Arnie says, 'I'll be Bach'".

Clunking his glass on the table Alan pulled on his SCO leather jacket and strode out the pub, humming, "Na, na, na, na, na America". As he turned left out of the pub door-way he thought to himself, "Bloody West Side Story, if you're not careful you'll be singing Bali Hai and all the bally rest."

Cassie was sitting in front of her screen as Alan took his jacket off and hung it on the back of his chair, before pulling a tie from his jacket pocket and putting it on. All the while humming, "Maria, I've just met a girl named Maria."

After the usual preliminaries from the Exchange of Information officers, Brad began the discussion by stating, "Yeheudah's attorney has been giving us the runaround." It was clear from the looks on both Brad and Leroy's faces that when Brad said, "Us," he meant Leroy. Brad continued, "I rang the guy yesterday and told him his client was in the last chance saloon, so we have a call booked for Wednesday next week."

"Did you get the Loan Application documents?" Cassie asked.

"Yes," replied Leroy, pleased to change the subject, "they state that Yeheudah lives in the UK and has a trade of being a property investor, isn't that against the law in England?"

"Yep", Alan responded, and realising that the Yanks might think that he was taking the piss, added, "obtaining money by deception."

"Covered by the Fraud Act now," Cassie added.

Alan nodded, but commented, "The old legislation did what it said on the tin."

Cassie, concerned that a Ronseal advert might not translate well over the pond, asked, "Are the Loan Applications useful to you?"

"Sure. I'm looking forward to our call next week," Brad commented.

It was agreed that they reconvene in three weeks' time, by which time the IRS's call would have taken place and Cassie would hope to have the mortgage applications from the lenders in respect of the other three properties and she was still waiting for bank statements for some of the accounts. The statements that had been received were far from exciting. There was no sign of where the money had come from to purchase the properties. They did show regular rents received from a letting agent and mortgage payments being made, Cassie though still hadn't received the company bank accounts and statements from MM Properties Limited.

Joe Goldsmith nervously clicked the onscreen button to connect him to the video call. There were three callers on the screen, the older of whom was already scowling at him.

"Is your client joining us today?" Brad asked. Knowing the answer before he asked the question.

"No," Joe replied, not wanting to fabricate an excuse.

Brad, not wishing to hear the excuse, simply said, "This is Anthony, one of our lawyers."

"Anthony, not Tony" thought Joe, "that tells me something."

Anthony began with a broadside. "Have you represented a client before involved in international tax fraud and money laundering?"

Joe knew that if he answered truthfully, "No," the implication was that he didn't know what he was doing and if he answered, "Yes," the IRS would suspect he was probably involved in some way himself. So, he answered the question with a question, "What makes you think my client has done anything wrong?"

Brad got a response in first, "Not turning up for this meeting."

Anthony then replied, "Failing to declare to the IRS that he has eight offshore companies, that's $80,000 US in penalties for a start."

Joe began to start in a mumble, "We are," and then got louder, "looking into that."

"You told me your client had nothing to do with the offshore companies and properties," Leroy stated.

Joe responded, "Yes, but…" and having failed to think of what to say next, "we are looking into that." Joe had never wished to be a politician, but right now he wished he had been as he couldn't think of what to say next. Unlike a politician. You know the kind of response that politicians come up with, "I am really glad you asked me that question." Translated as "That's just the question I didn't want you to ask."
Or, "Let me be clear about this" before waffling on and not answering the question.

Or, failing all that, "Good question, well asked. Next question."

The next question did come for Joe, this time from Anthony, "Where did your client get all the money from to buy all these properties in England?"
"There were some loans I understand," Joe replied.

"And what about the capital which wasn't borrowed from the financial institutions," Anthony continued.

"We are looking into that," Joe repeated.

"We are talking about millions of dollars," Anthony pointed out.

"Yes," Joe said, as he unconsciously nodded in agreement.

"That's a lot of polishing shoes," commented Brad.

"Shoe repairs," Joe corrected.

"Soles with holes," said Brad.

"Yes," Joe replied and trying to lighten the mood added, "sounds like one of those Methodist posters encouraging you to find God."

The humour fell on deaf ears and Brad warned, "Your client's story better not be full of holes when we summons him".

Anthony continued the attack, "Where does your client reside?"

Joe was pleased that he finally had a question he could reply to. "Although born in London my client is a US citizen and has lived in New York for over ten years."

"Why then, on these loan applications," Anthony held up the documents as he spoke, "does your client state he lives in England and, rather than having a shoe repair business, states that his trade is that of a property investor?"

"My client hasn't seen those documents," said Joe, quickly realising as he said the words he should have reworded the answer.

Sure enough, Brad picked up on this as he commented, "He has seen them alright, he's goddamned signed them."

Anthony interjected, "I think what Mr Goldsmith means is his client hasn't shown these documents to him." Joe nodded his head vigorously. Anthony continued, "Your client, Mr Goldsmith, has either committed offences in England by providing false information to the lenders, to obtain monies by deception, or he has lied to you and the IRS about residing in the USA. He has failed to declare to the IRS that he has eight offshore companies, making him liable to considerable penalties and, most serious of all, he has millions of dollars of unexplained cash invested in properties offshore. On the face of it he either has some sort of income he has not disclosed to the IRS, or it's not his money and he is laundering it for someone else. Either way it could mean jail time and we would ask that he tells us the truth." Anthony then paused before asking again, "Have you represented a client before involved in international tax fraud and money laundering?"

A defeated Joe Goldsmith replied, "No," and, after Brad had rammed it home that the IRS would be summonsing Yeheudah, Joe clicked the button enabling him to leave the meeting.

Although the meeting with the IRS had been a virtual one, sitting in his own office Joe felt a need to escape. So, he left the building in which his office sat and took a walk around the block. The cacophony of sound and the variety of smells, both good and bad, that assaulted his senses in a strange way relaxed him. Grabbing a coffee to go he returned to his office feeling really invigorated. He rang Yeheudah and arranged to see him first thing tomorrow. He was draining his coffee when his phone rang.

"Hello, Nigel Greenfield here," the voice on the phone said. "Just to let you know we are still investigating the matter."

To say Joe hadn't enjoyed being hauled over the coals by the IRS was an understatement, so to have this English guy give him the runaround really stuck in his craw. What sort of a schmuck did he take him for. So he replied, "My client is a poor shoe repairer, he has no property, no companies and no loans. So I suggest you get your head out of your client's butt and get him to sort this shit out."

"I'll see what I can do," Nigel Greenfield replied.

"You'd better be quicker than shit through a goose, because the IRS is going to summons my client".

Nigel Greenfield replied, "Oh," but Joe had already put the phone down.

Nigel Greenfield's first thought was, "What do I do now?" At least in the UK HMRC couldn't force a client to a meeting, unless it was a criminal investigation, and then they could answer "No comment" to each question. This was an IRS summons, this was different. You couldn't just not turn up and you couldn't "No comment," unless you wanted to risk ending up getting arrested. Nigel Greenfield didn't like his clients to meet HMRC if he could help it. Too much chance of them telling the truth or, more likely, telling a lie which didn't fit in with the lies told by another of his clients. Percival Parrott hadn't even got back to him. He decided he would call Percival until he got a response.

Percival Parrott was sitting on the veranda of his villa in Eilat. He had just enjoyed a sumptuous meal and was letting it settle into his large belly. As he took a long draw on his Romeo and Juliet cigar and sipped his Henessy five-star brandy, he looked out to sea where the occasional lights of the boats twinkled like stars low on the horizon. This moment of tranquility was disturbed by his phone ringing. He answered it gruffly, without even bothering to look at the caller's name. The fact that it was Nigel Greenfield did nothing to improve his mood. He had glanced at Cassie's letter earlier which Nigel Greenfield had emailed to him, but had concluded, why should I bother doing anything?

"Have you any advice on what we should do next as the IRS is about to summons my client's cousin?" Nigel Greenfield asked.

"Am I in any way involved in this one?" was Percival Parrot's first question and when Nigel Greenfield replied, "No," he went on to ask, "Does your client intend to leave London and, if so, does he need my help to set up in Israel?"

"Not as yet," Nigel Greenfield replied.

"Well, for now I think you need to sort out the mess you created," said Percival Parrott and, with synchronised motions, clicked his phone with his thumb ending the call, bringing the cigar to his mouth for another long draw and, with his other hand, raised the glass to take yet another sip of the brandy.

Nigel Greenfield thought to himself, "I need to ring Mossi," and then he thought, "It could wait until tomorrow."

Joe's first client that morning was Yeheudah. Yeheudah sat opposite Joe, his left hand on his knee, clenched in fear and anger, his right hand in Sarah's vice-like grip. Despite being sat in separate chairs, it seemed to Joe that Yeheudah and Sarah couldn't possibly be any closer together. Sarah was like a limpet on Yeheudah, but Yeheudah was presently feeling like limp seaweed on a beach, rather than the rock. Joe was explaining what had happened with the IRS yesterday and he had got to the part of the conversation he had been dreading.

"The IRS is going to summons you to a meeting. You are going to need a top tax attorney and that's not me. I have never dealt with an overseas tax fraud case like this, I can put you in touch with some top firms in Manhattan but I warn you their hourly rates will make your eyes water.

"But he's done nothing wrong," Sarah cried.

Joe thought to himself, "Yes he has, he signed those documents," but he said nothing, keeping what he hoped was an empathetic face. Yeheudah moved his left hand from his knee and placed it on Sarah's hand, "Can you select the best of these top firms and ask them to ring me?" he asked.

"Of course," Joe replied.

Rachel Greenfield was chatting away to her husband Nigel relating to him a conversation she had had with their neighbour about their respective eldest sons' educations. Their neighbour's son was doing his Masters at Oxford in relation to Particle Physics. Their son has switched courses from Applied Mathematics to Sociology and currently seemed more interested in becoming a stand-up comedian. Her husband though had not responded, nor had he moved. It was most unusual to see him still sitting at the table when she came to clear away the breakfast things. Seeing the pensive look on his face she said nothing. She saw her husband look at his watch and, like a schoolboy called to the Headmaster's office, he got up and walked incredibly slowly to the door.

After a very slow walk Greenfield had reached the office. A quarter of an hour later he was still sitting at his desk staring into space. He had eventually walked to the electrical cabinet, retrieved the phone which he used to call Mossi and pressed the call button. Before he spoke, he looked down at his groin imagining what could happen to his manhood if he upset Mossi.

Then he said, "Mossi, there is nothing I can do, you need to convince your cousin to play ball."

There was no response from Mossi other than a low growl, before he hung up.

Afterwards Greenfield felt relieved. The rest of the day continued as normal. At about 11 o'clock Rachel rang him, ostensibly to ask him to pick up some bits for tea on his way back from the office, but actually to check that he was ok.

At the end of the day Greenfield picked up a piece of paper from his desk on which he had written the list of ingredients his wife had asked him to pick up. He put it in the top pocket of his suit jacket and, collecting his coat from the stand, he placed it over his arm as he locked up the office.

The shop his wife wished him to visit was just three doors down from his office. He had just stepped through the doorway when he was shoved in the back, his nose smacked against the sign that read, 'Best Bagels in London.' When he staggered back, his nose bleeding, he had left a red mark on the sign.

Mossi stepped into the shop, locking the door behind him. When Greenfield had entered the shop five seconds earlier two staff members had been standing behind the counter. Now, like the shop assistant in Mr Benn in reverse, they had disappeared. Greenfield then found himself spun around, his neck being squeezed by Mossi's right hand.

"I don't believe there is nothing you can do," said Mossi.

Greenfield looked into Mossi's eyes. It reminded him of his childhood. They had lived by the sea, he and his brother had been fishing trying to catch bass or pollock, all they had caught were three dogfish. There had been disappointment in his mother's eyes that there was no edible fish to add to their meagre evening meal, but it wasn't the disappointed eyes of his mother that Greenfield was looking into, it was the eyes of the dead dogfish.

"There isn't," Greenfield spluttered as Mossi's hand now squeezed his throat even harder, "not without your cousin's co-operation."

"And, if he does?" said Mossi, slightly loosening his grip on Greenfield's throat.

"If your cousin admits the properties are his to the IRS, we can create some inheritance from Israel. Together with letters regarding a disputed will, which can explain why the properties were purchased in London, not New York, in order to hide having invested the inheritance from the other claimants. He will have some penalties to pay which you could cover for him."

"What about the mortgages?" Mossi demanded. "Has anyone from our Community ever gone to prison for mortgage fraud?" Greenfield responded, with more confidence than he felt.

"But what if he grasses?" Mossi quite literally spat out the last word.

Greenfield thought about wiping the spit from his face, but the trickle of blood from his nose reminded him the best move was not to move. Taking a deep breath Greenfield replied, "I have spoken to Percival Parrott about this. If your cousin does finger you, you might want to spend some time in our very own Costa Del Crime, by becoming a Red Sea recluse. You know Israel won't extradite you to the UK for mere tax fraud."

"You were right," said Mossi, adding, as he lifted Greenfield off the ground and threw him through some neatly stacked shelves of tinned Kosher goods, "you can't help me." Having heard the shop door being unlocked and swung open the two shop assistants nervously reappeared. One of them helped Greenfield to his feet and then asked, "What can I get for you?" Greenfield pulled the shopping list from the top pocket of his now dishevelled suit jacket.

Yeheudah and Sarah, after meeting with Joe, had spent the rest of the day discussing what Yeheudah should do about the situation. By that evening Sarah had convinced Yeheudah that he should tell the truth. Mossi had always scared Yeheudah but, thought Yeheudah, what could be scarier than life without Sarah? Other than perhaps the thought of Sarah and his children trying to survive without the money he brought into the household. Yeheudah and Sarah spent the night cuddled together, like a condemned man spending a last few hours with his wife before giving himself up.

The next day Yeheudah had begun to get ready for work, but Sarah had insisted that, for today at least, he stay at home with her. They were still sitting later that day at the kitchen table, holding hands, when Yeheudah's phone began to ring. Sarah looked at the phone as if she had never seen a phone ring before. Yeheudah, not recognising the number, answered the phone.

The one-sided conversation that Sarah heard was, "Mossi," in a voice most unlike her husband's, it was of a much higher pitch, almost female. The startled voice continued, "Yes Mossi." "I know Mossi." "But my attorney says." "Yes Mossi." "But jail time Mossi."

Sarah had heard enough, she grabbed the phone from Yeheudah and screamed into it, "He's not going to jail for you and if he doesn't tell the IRS the truth, I will." She hung up and stared at Yeheudah, her eyes ablaze. Yeheudah knew that stare. It had happened only once before in their marriage when one of the Community Leaders had clipped their six year old son around the ear, having tripped over the six year old, when their son had run in front of the Community Leader, he had only been playing with another child. Sarah had picked up their son in one arm and smacked the leader across the face with her free hand. The whole room was shocked, but Yeheudah, seeing his wife's blazing eyes, had not dared to say anything to her. She had been like a lioness protecting her young.

Yeheudah looked at his phone on the kitchen table, knowing that his wife had shown her claws again, but this time to the wrong man because he knew that, "You don't mess with Mossi".

CHAPTER FOURTEEN

Cassie and her colleagues filed into the meeting room for their monthly management meeting which Alan chaired. Senior management would select each month certain topics for the team to discuss.

Alan's meetings were called team meetings, as Alan didn't like to be called a manager. As he said himself, "Manager sounds like I am just managing, or that you lot are such lazy gits that I need to manage you. I am not a manager, I am your operational leader." Alan was a leader, mentor and proud, caring father to his team.

Usually, the topics of discussion selected by senior management were dealt with by Alan as follows.

"This month we are required to discuss coaching, diversity and whistleblowers. Well, we all know that Rovers need a new coach. Diversity is a Welsh poet who writes about Bristol's other football team and whistleblowing is what the referee does at the end of the match. So, we can record in the minutes that we have discussed them all."

But on this occasion Carl piped up, "I would like to discuss whistleblowers. Where my wife works there was a whistleblower who was telling the truth, but instead of heads rolling amongst senior management, they just found some scapegoat to pin it on."

Now where Cassie grew up people just got on with their lives. People didn't talk about scapegoats, so it wasn't a phrase she had ever heard before.

So, in response to Carl's statement she said, "These escape goats".

The team all laughed but there was no malice, it was more a case of "Oh, that's our Cassie."
Alan had his own mental image of Cassie's escape goat that made him chuckle. A goat on a motorbike, dressed in a German soldier's uniform, was being chased by German soldiers, also on motorbikes. The goat attempts to jump the wire fence into neutral Switzerland, on his motorbike, but ends up entangled in the wire. Or is that just, "A Great Escape-goat."

The meeting moved on to more important topics. Of how much yield was required to hit this year's target and when was the next team social.

After the meeting ended, Alan called Cassie over to his desk.

"How's that Polish case of yours?" Alan asked.

"Polish?" Cassie replied, not for the first time not knowing what Alan was on about.

"Moskovitch", Alan clarified.

"He's British, but I assume with Polish forebears," Cassie replied.

"He's got one more than Goldilocks then," Alan joked, before adding, "so how's it going?"

"I've had responses from all of the financial institutions now. All of the mortgages show Yeheudah as the borrower and he has declared that he resides in the UK and trades as a property investor. We have the bank statements for the bank accounts of the eight companies. There is nothing that stands out from these, apart from the account of MM Properties Limited. The other companies' bank accounts show rents coming in from a letting agent and the mortgage payments going out. MM Properties Limited's bank account however, shows cash banked and mortgage payments paid out. So, we are really waiting for the IRS to summons Yeheudah and hear his explanation of the millions of pounds required to purchase the eight properties, over and above the mortgages we have identified."

"What was the last news you received from over the pond?" Alan asked.

"Yeheudah's tax attorney has dropped him as a client," Cassie replied.

"Seems like the Tax Advisor could've been legit," Cassie added.

"You mean kosher but, joking aside, we could do with more honest tax advisors in this investigation, not less, and the IRS still doesn't have a date set for the meeting they are summonsing Yeheudah to attend," said Alan. Cassie nodded in agreement.

"So, you've got some time on your hands?" Alan beamed. Cassie knew that face and knew it meant more work.

"We've got a new trainee joining us," Alan continued. He's a bit wet behind the yers, as they say in Wales, but with a good investigator to guide him he'll be alright."
"I am a good investigator?" said Cassie, more of a query than a statement. Alan replied, "Yes, I know you are and Jacob will learn a lot from you. What's more," he added, "this month I will report you're mentoring, next month I will report that you are

coaching him. So that's two boxes ticked for me. I have arranged for you both to go out on a Knock so he can see that criminal investigation work is not all, 'Get your trousers on you're nicked, we're the Sweeney and we haven't had our breakfast'".

Cassie had seen the Sweeney when she had been channel hopping and agreed with Alan's view of going on a Knock. Five minutes of potential excitement, followed by hours of logging evidence. Then, before getting to trial, disclosing hundreds if not thousands of documents to the other side. All of which had to be meticulously recorded and logged so that they could be tracked from the Knock all the way to the trial. After all this, there was always the chance that the Crown Prosecution Service might decide not to proceed with the prosecution.

The next day Cassie got to meet Jacob. He was a slim, bright, intelligent young man. He had joined HMRC straight from University but, most importantly, he seemed very keen to learn.

The training team had selected the income tax returns of two Traders for him to open enquiries into. One was a newsagent in Newport, South Wales. The other ran a pub in Notting Hill in London.

First of all, there was the Knock that Alan had arranged for them both to go out on. Thankfully for Cassie it was in Bristol so it wouldn't require her getting up at 3 am or something stupid. Cassie and Jacob had spent the previous day with their criminal investigation colleagues. Jenny, who was leading the Knock, explained the investigation so far. A VAT officer had visited the Trader, Dicky Yorath. Whilst checking the purchase invoices in support of the input VAT claimed, the officer had identified potential fraudulent invoices. The officer had then advised Dicky Yorath that she needed to carry out some further checks on his VAT return and so she would be taking away his VAT records for that quarter. Visits had been made by HMRC officers to the three suppliers which the suspected invoices reported to have originated from. Each of the suppliers had confirmed that the invoices taken from Dicky Yorath by the HMRC officer had not been produced by them and Jenny had gone before a magistrate who had authorised a search warrant. The criminal investigation team weren't expecting any trouble from Dicky Yorath, but the local police had been alerted as to what was happening and the potential for HMRC to need assistance.

Observations had been carried out to establish Dicky Yorath's pattern of life from which it had been learned that Dicky Yorath's two children caught the school bus at 0830, so the Knock was planned to go in at 0845.

Jacob was tense as he sat there in the car in his HMRC stab vest waiting for the words, "Go, go, go". Cassie, meanwhile, was cold. She had asked the criminal investigations officer if he could start the car and turn the heating on. He replied he didn't want to give their position away.

"Is he for real?" she thought. "He's CI not CI5. How I wish I had my hot water bottle, no-one would notice it under this stab vest. I hope the house we're knocking has central heating."

Ten minutes later the words, "Go, go, go," came over the Criminal Investigation Officer's mobile. Jacob's hand was on the door handle in a flash.

"Sit down," boomed the Criminal Investigations Officer and then, in a voice like a school teacher instructing his class the bell is a signal for me not for you, he said, "You're Civil, you go in last."

The Knock, when it went in, could not have been more straightforward. After Dicky Yorath had opened the door, he had straight away realised what was going on and it was with an air of resignation that he had fully opened the door and read the search warrant that had been handed to him. It hadn't been necessary to caution Dicky Yorath, this clearly wasn't his first rodeo. By the time Cassie and Jacob eventually entered the building all this was done and dusted and Dicky Yorath was asking the officers whether they wanted tea or coffee. A hot drink sounded like heaven to Cassie's cold bones. The feeling that Dicky Yorath saw arrest as an occupational hazard was somewhat tempered by the sound of his wife weeping in the living room. Cassie could hear Ronnie Barker's voice as the judge from an old TV programme that had come to her attention when the teachers at her school had discovered, to their great amusement, that the boy who sat in front of her in class, Duncan Fletcher, had a Dad called Norman Stanley Fletcher.

Following the officers in front of them, Cassie and Jacob found themselves in what had been the dining room, but was now serving as Dicky Yorath's office. The laborious task of logging and bagging the evidence began. The only break in this monotony being when Jacob picked up Dicky Yorath's passport and, showing what Cassie thought were promising investigating skills, started checking the stamps and visas to check where Dicky had been travelling. Only for Dicky Yorath to shout at him, "That's not covered by the search warrant". Jacob dropped the passport, like a teenage boy caught by his Mum with a porn mag. A couple of the older officers laughed and Jenny reminded the team to stick to the terms of the search warrant.

The Knock had gone in at 0845. It was now 1645 and, despite a number of cups of Dicky Yorath's coffee, Cassie could see that Jacob's eyes were glazing over. Someone had mentioned going back to the office for more evidence bags so Cassie hitched a lift for her and Jacob back to the office. Cassie asked Jenny if she could keep Jacob and herself up to date with the investigation as it progressed.

When they got back to the office Alan was waiting and beckoned them over. Alan asked how it had gone and Cassie replied, pointing out in particular Dicky Yorath's nonchalance.

Alan then turned to Jacob and asked, "How do you like criminal work?" Jacob was still trying to think of how to respond when Alan added, "Fucking boring ain't it?" Jacob nodded.
Cassie smiled knowing that she had rarely heard Alan swear and, when she had, Alan had not been swearing in anger but, as on this occasion, the swearing had been in order to place emphasis on a particular word.

The next day she helped Jacob draft his letters opening the inquiries into the Income Tax Returns of the publican in Notting Hill, Winston Walker, and the newsagent in Newport, Imran Ali.

CHAPTER FIFTEEN

Mossi's phone call to Yeheudah not having worked led Mossi to decide that a more hands on approach was required. He was booked on a flight to New York and was waiting in the departure lounge bar for his flight number on the screen to show "Go To Gate". All of the tables in the bar were occupied but Mossi's table was the only table with a single occupant, no-one having dared to join him at his table. The screen changed and "Go To Gate 12," appeared on the screen. Mossi drained his glass of San Miguel and, as he rose from his chair turning to face the opening in the furniture that acted as a wall to this departure lounge bar, a race began between two families wanting to grab his table for themselves. So it was that a game of musical chairs, without the music, began. The first family to move was a family of four who looked like they'd walked off the set of 'Ask The Family'. "Question for mother and youngest child." But it was a family of considerable girth to their frames who got there first by preventing access, with their sheer size, to the father and older child from the 'Ask The Family' family, whilst the competing family's child waddled to victory, claiming a seat at the table after a blocking move worthy of the Kansas City Chiefs.

Mossi, oblivious to the race, walked swiftly to the gate. When he arrived, there was already a bit of commotion. The airline staff had announced that the flight was oversubscribed, making the airline's attempt to maximise profits seem like a Readers Digest' order. As the staff worked their way down the queue seeking a volunteer to catch a later flight Mossi could hear snatches of the conversation. The airline staff came up to a smartly dressed couple. The man announced, "We will be on this flight". The airline staff replied they couldn't guarantee that, to which the man responded, "If we are not on the flight there will be a Writ on your Managing Director's desk in the morning." The airline staff moved on down the queue. The scowl on Mossi's face when the staff drew near to him made them move swiftly on. A little further down the line two lads in rugby tops negotiated £50 each to wait three hours in the bar for a later flight.

Mossi boarded the plane. Once at his seat he placed his coat, as he had no luggage, in the overhead locker. He took the window seat. The young pimply faced man, whose seat this was, was a late arrival. The young man had already had to squeeze past the woman in the outside seat who was deep in conversation with her friend sitting across the aisle. The man sat in front of Mossi reclined his seat and, just as the pimply faced young man was getting to what should have been Mossi's seat, Mossi stood up, leaned over the seat in front and said, "If you fucking recline your seat again I'll break your fucking neck".

The pimply faced young man decided to sit in the middle seat, the boarding pass he had held in his right hand ready to remonstrate with Mossi for being sat in his seat he tucked into his shirt pocket. He grabbed the inflight catalogue and began to flick through it pretending he hadn't heard what Mossi had said. Neither he nor the man sitting in front of Mossi barely moved a muscle during the entire flight. The plane landed at JFK airport and, after clearing US customs, it wasn't long before Mossi was in the back of Mikey Keane's yellow cab. Mikey Keane had shrugged his shoulders when Mossi had given his location as the Astoria Hotel. "A guy off a long-distance flight with no luggage and he was heading straight for a dive full of hookers and low-lifes, New York New York, it's a hell of a town."

Mossi knew the Astoria well, but he hadn't directed the cab there because he wanted a hooker, but because it was part of his Modus Operandi, never leaving a trail of breadcrumbs for the cops to follow. Too many crooks got caught because they were lazy. Mossi rarely would get off a bus where he actually wanted to go, taxis likewise. He would rather walk a short distance and conceal his movements. So, knowing the Astoria was two blocks away from Yeheudah's apartment, he had directed the cab driver there. If all went well, he might treat himself at the Astoria on the way back.

"What was the name of the girl last time?" he couldn't remember at first and then the memory came back to him. 'Glenda the Gannet', that's what he'd called her, after she had finished the breakfast he had bought her the following morning like someone who hadn't eaten for weeks. By the time he had finished recollecting his night with Glenda, Mossi had arrived at Yeheudah and Sarah's apartment.

Mossi banged on the front door, the way he did when he had been debt collecting. Yeheudah opened the door but kept the chain on. Mossi took this as an insult and, with well-practised ease, barged the door open leaving the chain dangling from the door with the two insufficient screws that had been securing the chain to the door frame, swinging in the air like decorations.

"Aren't you going to invite me in cousin? I've been looking forward to playing some games with your kids," Mossi said with the falsest of smiles. Yeheudah shuddered to think what games Mossi had in mind. Yeheudah led Mossi from the small hallway into the kitchen. Sarah had already positioned herself by the door in the kitchen leading to the children's bedrooms.

Mossi began the conversation, "All you need to do is to admit the properties are yours."

"I don't want to go to jail," Yeheudah pleaded.

"You won't," Mossi explained, "we will invent an inheritance to explain where the money came from and any tax and penalties the IRS charges you I'll pay."

"And what about the loan fraud in England?" Yeheudah demanded.

"I'll deal with it," Mossi replied and then, as an afterthought, added, "and I'll give you $50,000 US."

"Don't listen to him, you'll end up in jail," Sarah shrieked.

Bolstered by his wife's resolve Yeheudah said defiantly, "I'm not going to jail."

"It seems I need to cut your brats," Mossi said, finding the largest kitchen knife from the block and swinging the knife in Yeheudah's direction.

Yeheudah saw Sarah out of the corner of his eye and realised that, on hearing the words "your brats," Sarah intended to throw herself at Mossi. So Yeheudah stepped forward so he could swing out his left arm to impede Sarah's lunge towards Mossi. Yeheudah's step forward brought him into the arc of Mossi's arm and the knife sliced through Yeheudah's neck, cutting the carotid artery. As Yeheudah fell to the floor blood sprayed the kitchen wall like a Karcher power washer. Sarah dropped to her knees beside her husband, desperately trying to stem the blood. Mossi had brought the knife to his side and let it slip from his hand. The knife landed point first, piercing the linoleum and embedding itself in the floorboard below. Mossi had considered killing Sarah and the brats but it was logic, not compassion, that saved them as, in that split second, Mossi had dismissed this course of action as taking too long. Particularly with the thin walls in this shabby apartment the neighbours would be alerted that something was wrong.

Mossi turned around and left the kitchen. In the small hallway stood a full-length mirror, Sarah would use it to check before leaving the house that she was not wearing anything that would cause offense to their community. Despite wearing a wig to cover her hair from the eyes of other men she would still check that there were no strands of false hair escaping from her hat. Mossi checked himself in the mirror. There was blood on his coat and on his right hand. He wiped his hand on his coat and then, taking off his coat, he folded it up and put it over his arm.

Last night Yeheudah had held Sarah in his arms, now she cradled his dead body in hers weeping uncontrollably.

Mossi, having arrived at Yeheudah's apartment from due south, now headed west. After he had walked about three blocks he saw a homeless drunk asleep in a shop doorway. Mossi knelt down beside the drunk and, lifting the drunk's head, placed his coat as a pillow below it. Without even opening his eyes the drunk snuggled down into his new found pillow. After another two blocks Mossi saw another yellow cab and hailed it. About the same time Sarah, surrounded by her children and their neighbours, had with the help of the neighbours rung the police, Mossi was on his way to JFK airport. By the time the police arrived at Sarah's apartment Mossi was at JFK airport purchasing a ticket. Two hours later, according to the flight manifest, Avi Klein was sitting in seat 32a bound for Geneva.

Running on adrenaline, nine hours later Mossi took a train from Geneva to Zurich. In Zurich he went shopping, cash of course, buying two suits, five shirts, three ties, a coat, a pair of shoes and new underwear. He dumped his old clothes in a skip he found down an alley adjacent to the shop. By now he was tired, very tired and, as David Goldman, he checked into the Hotel Excelsior Zurich.

The next morning, having slept in till nine, Mossi felt refreshed and he ordered from room service a breakfast of cold meats, cheeses and egg with a large pot of coffee. After showering and shaving he wrapped himself in one of the hotel's very soft dressing gowns. Whilst eating his breakfast he rang his bank in Zurich advising them he required access today to his safety deposit box. Mossi put on the fresh shirt and suit that he had bought the day before. In the hotel lobby was a shop selling designer suitcases. He was a shop assistant's dream, the suitcases were overpriced and the assistant's basic salary was boosted by commission. Mossi simply walked into the shop and, before the shop assistant could start her sales patter, he pointed at the suitcase he wanted. Mossi took the suitcase back to his room, packed his new clothes and all of the toiletries in the bathroom then left the suitcase with the concierge.

Mossi walked to the bank. The bank looked more like an office than a bank, there were no bank tellers behind glass or cashpoint machines, just a reception desk and a waiting area. Once his identity had been verified, Mossi was escorted by a smartly dressed young woman to a small room with no windows and only one way in. The young woman left and, a few minutes later, an equally well-dressed young man brought in his box pointing to the button on the small desk in the centre of the room which Mossi was to ring when he was ready to return the box. The box was made of stainless steel and had a digital keypad for the entry of the four digit combination.

Mossi entered the digits 6.6.6, he liked people to be scared of him so why not, he then entered the digit 1 for the man he had killed. Smiling to himself he thought, "I'll need to change that to 6.6.6.2."

The safety deposit box was Mossi's emergency going away kit. He unwrapped from a gun oil cloth, an automatic. He wouldn't be needing it this time but who knows how long it would be before he would next have access to the box so he skilfully dismantled the Sig Sauer P320 and, using the cleaning kit which was also in the box, he spent the next ten minutes cleaning, oiling and reassembling the ten millimetre automatic. He then wrapped the automatic in the gun oil cloth again and replaced it in the box. Mossi had never yet had to shoot anyone but, when he did, he wanted them to stay dead, hence his decision to buy a 10 millimetre rather than the usual 9 millimetre. He took bundles of $100 US bills and 50 Euro notes and stuffed them in the deep pockets of his new suit jacket, a suit jacket he had chosen for this purpose rather than for any sartorial elegance. Despite the large amount of cash now stuffed in his pockets, this was just spending money. The real valuables were in two black velvet bags in the safety deposit box. One bag contained uncut diamonds, the other black pearls. He slipped the bags into the left and right inside pockets of his jacket and then he zipped them shut. Mossi wouldn't be taking this jacket off in a hurry. He rang the bell. The smartly dressed young man collected his safety deposit box and the smartly dressed young woman escorted him back to reception. Mossi walked back to the Excelsior Hotel and collected his luggage. He then walked for five minutes before spotting a taxi rank and took a taxi to the airport. A few hours later David Goldman sat in seat 16b from Zurich to Dubai for catching a flight to Abu Dhabi.

CHAPTER SIXTEEN

Sarah Rosental had told the cops about the eight properties registered in her husband's name that were actually owned by Mossi. The New York Police Department had contacted the IRS the following morning. The NYPD had also contacted the FBI who, in turn, had contacted the Metropolitan Police in London. It, however, took a further fortnight for Cassie and Alan to learn what had happened. They had been pressing the IRS for another video call as they wanted to know if Yeheudah had been summonsed to a meeting and, if so, what explanation he had given about the eight London properties purchased in his name.

When the video conference call did happen it was different from the previous calls. Leroy was missing and in his place was a woman who introduced herself as Connie Wong attorney, rather than Connie Wong, attorney. The attorney then did all of the talking during what was a very short call. The attorney spoke lawyer-speak fluently. Slightly different from British lawyer-speak, but lawyer-speak all the same. The facts that Alan and Cassie gathered from Connie Wong attorney were that Mossi had murdered Yeheudah, Mossi was on the run, HMRC were to do nothing and, if HMRC learned anything about Mossi's whereabouts, they were to tell the IRS straight away. Then, almost as though the attorney had been forced to reveal the fact, she advised that Yeheudah's widow had confirmed that the eight properties were Mossi's. What wasn't said was that Brad looked most unhappy about the whole thing.

Alan looked at Cassie and said, "We need a proper conversation about this and I am buying."

Alan chose The Bridge, a pub with a very impressive mural of Jimmi Hendrix, but not a huge amount of room inside. All the same, Alan and Cassie found a table.

"Brad looked bloody miserable," said Alan.

"He didn't get a chance to charge Yeheudah the $80,000 US penalties" Cassie replied.

"Always charge the penalties if chummy's looking peaky," Alan commented.

Cassie nodded and smiled knowingly. You can't charge a dead man penalties but, get those penalties out before he croaks and the penalties can be paid out of the estate.

"I am having those properties," Cassie stated defiantly, taking a sip of her wine, as if to reinforce her statement.

Alan smiled proudly and replied, "I thought you would."

Cassie set out her plan to raise Discovery Income Tax Assessments on Mossi, based on the deposits required to fund the purchase of the properties. She would also charge penalties and she intended to bankrupt Mossi and to work with the Proceeds of Crime team and the Insolvency Service to recover HMRC's debt by selling the properties. Cassie also advised Alan of her intention to contact the Metropolitan Police, via HMRC's liaison officer, regarding the mortgage frauds.

"I can just imagine the trial," said Alan.

Mossi's defence counsel: "There is no evidence of my client's connection to these mortgage frauds. All of the evidence points towards them having been committed by Yeheudah Rosenthal."

Judge: "Where is Yeheudah Rosenthal?"

King's Counsel: "Dead M'Lord."

Judge: "Where is Mossi Moscovitch?"

King's Counsel: "Currently on the Federal Bureau of Investigations' Most Wanted list, suspected of murdering the aforementioned Yeheudah Rosenthal, M'Lord."

Over the next couple of days Cassie issued the Income Tax Discovery Assessments and Penalties Explanation letters to Mossi.

As no reply was received the Penalty Assessments were issued. Mossi had thirty days to appeal.

Neither Winston Walker nor Imran Ali had responded to Jacob's enquiry letters. Jacob had issued four more Information Notices to both Traders, pleased to have received Cassie's advice not to incorporate their request for documents and information into his enquiry letters, but instead to have listed the documents and information he required on separate schedules as Jacob could not reuse those schedules to accompany a formal Information Notice.

That was four weeks ago now. Alan had noticed that Cassie was spending every lunch time searching online for Mossi. Cassie being so fit and slim she felt the cold more than most, certainly more than Alan, for whom forty years of drinking beer had provided a layer of fat to protect him from the cold. Cassie would usually at lunchtime be refilling her hot water bottle but Alan had noticed she hadn't been doing that these past few weeks. He was concerned about her and decided to do something about it. Alan didn't normally do 'one to ones'. Explaining, "I speak to my investigators every day," but he had informed Cassie that they would be having a one to one in his own inimitable way.

He walked over to Cassie's desk about 2pm and said, "Lovely day for a walk, get your coat on and let's go."

It was a lovely day for a walk, sunny, no wind and not too cold, when you were well wrapped up.

"I know he may be Cassie's Mossi wanted, but you can give it a rest now and again," Alan said.

"I know, but I just want to find the bastard," Cassie replied with feeling.

"I am not saying stop, just that a change is as good as a rest," Alan commented.

They had arrived at their destination, The Barley Mow. Cassie sat at a table and opened her purse.

Alan waved her purse away explaining, "This is a one to one and that could be conceived as bribery, so I'll get the drinks, Sauvignon Blanc is it?" Cassie nodded.

Alan returned a few minutes later with Cassie's glass of wine and a pint of this week's guest ale, Swordfish. Sitting down he sipped his beer smiling, pleased at his choice. Then he said, "Jacob has received the publican's business records. I saw him earlier with the familiar look on his face of an investigator with their first lot of records."

"Oh yes, the 'What-the-hell-do-I-do-now' look," Cassie replied.

"That's the one, think you could give him a hand?" Alan asked.

"Of course," said Cassie.

"I suppose I should ask you where you would like to see yourself in five years' time" asked Alan.

"On a beach, in the Maldives, after winning the lottery," joked Cassie.

"Where do you see yourself going work wise?" asked Alan.

"Nowhere, I like it where I am," Cassie replied honestly.

"You're wrong about going nowhere, because you're coming to Jill's Britvic birthday do next Friday," Alan ordered.

"Britvic birthday?" Cassie queried.

"Britvic 55" Alan explained.

"So, order from your OL, you only play 'Where's Mossi' every other lunchtime and you keep your hot water bottle hot, deal?"

"Deal," said Cassie, grateful that Alan had told her what she had been unsuccessful in telling herself. Don't obsess about Mossi.
Alan sipped his Swordfish, placing his glass back on the table with a satisfied, "Aaahhh".

The next day Cassie saw Jacob come into the office and, after he had sat down and logged in, she walked over to his desk.

"I hear you have the records in for your publican?" Cassie stated.

"Yes, came in by drop box yesterday," Jacob replied.

"Where do you start?" Cassie asked. Jacob's expression spoke volumes. It didn't matter if the records were electronic or came in a carrier bag, how had the figures declared on the tax return been arrived at from these records? Jacob hadn't got to that point yet.

"So, first you need to establish how the figures declared were arrived at from the records provided. If you're not able to do so, you need the documents or information from the accountant to show you how he or she has arrived at them," Cassie explained.

The following day Jacob proudly announced he knew how the figures were arrived at. Cassie asked him to show her and, once he had done so, Cassie smiled and said, "Now we will find out what the taxable profits really are. Analyse the sales week by week into a graph."

Later that morning Jacob emailed Cassie the results of his analysis. There was an increase in sales in the summer and a small further increase for the

Notting Hill Carnival. Cassie told Jacob what she thought.

"There is a small rise in sales for the carnival but not as big as I would have expected. We will need to interview the Trader about that. How are you on Business Economics?" Cassie asked.

"We covered it in theory and on exercise examples in training, but I have not dealt with it in practice," Jacob replied. What HMRC calls Business Economics involves calculating the profits actually being made by business, such as a pub, from its purchases. The Inland Revenue's use of Business Economics in the 1980s had come as a shock to the publicans of Bristol. Two particular tax inspectors had concentrated on pubs. They had selected pubs whose accounts declared low gross profit rates and carried out a business economics exercise to calculate what the true profits were. They would then meet with the Trader in the pub and, over a pint, would ascertain how much money he had and how much money he could raise. They would then inform the Trader how much tax and penalties they could assess based on the Business Economics exercise and they would then agree to a letter of offer from him, for a smaller sum, that cleaned him out, but didn't bankrupt him.

Publicans got wise to this and would suppress purchases to increase their gross profit rates and/or they inflate their wastage, ie, the beer loss, when serving customers, cleaning the pipes, etc. which would also increase their GPR.

It was useful therefore when investigating a pub to know about how to run a pub. Cassie had grown up in a pub. Her parents' pub had been tied to a brewery and one of her Dad's priorities had been to ensure that the brewery didn't take too much of their hard earned profits. For example, the brewery required its landlords to sell its own blended whisky as the basic whisky. The brewery charged the landlords more for a bottle of their whisky than a better-quality blended whisky, such as Teachers, could be bought for from Tesco. The bottle of whisky with the brewery's label on it behind her parents' bar would, therefore, often actually contain Teachers' whisky bought at Tesco. As to tax, rules were bent. For example, Wilfred, their border collie who wouldn't hurt a fly, was apparently a guard dog whose food was claimed as tax deductible.

Cassie, not surprisingly, enjoyed investigating pubs. The first thing she would do would be to check what stock was behind the bar and compare this to what was on the purchase invoices supporting the VAT return. The Trader's would be wide eyed when the first question from this young VAT girl was, "Where did you get the Magners cider from, because it's not on the purchase invoices that you have given to me?"

Or, when an accountant had advised his client to inflate the wastage of beer lost when cleaning the pipes, only for Cassie to ask, "You clean the pipes once a week, you have four pumps with 20' of ¾" piping running from the barrels in the cellar, through double flash coolers, so how many pints are wasted cleaning these pipes?"

There was also the question of how much the trader drank of his or her own beer. Cassie had once interviewed a publican and asked him how much of his beer he had drunk. The accountant replied for him, "Twenty pints a week". Only for the publican to correct his accountant and say, "No, twenty pints a day." Which led to the conversation between the publican and the accountant, "I thought it was twenty pints a week?"

"No twenty pints a day. It's not a lot really, I start when I'm opening up in the morning and I have my last pint about 1am when I'm cleaning up after shut tap."

A nice adjustment to taxable profits. "I will drink to that," thought Cassie.

Jacob had completed his Business Economics exercise as best as he could from the business records provided. If there were omitted sales then they weren't arising from these purchase invoices. He had found some small sums of personal expenditure put through the accounts as business expenditure, "Dog food for Wilfred" thought Cassie.

A meeting at the pub was arranged. Just as Cassie and Jacob arrived at the pub the heavens opened. Cassie put up her brolly and was grateful when the door opened. Winston Walker welcomed them in and introduced them to his accountant, Vince Abbott.

They shook hands. Winston Walker's handshake was firm and friendly. Vince Abbott's was sloppy.

Whenever Cassie shook hands, she always thought of what her Dad had taught her from his Royal Navy days, "Sloppy salute, sloppy handshake, sloppy man."

Cassie recalled the pub that she had grown up in when she lived in Pembrokeshire. The beer garden had once been home to pigs and, running alongside it, was a pretty little brook which gave the pub its name. The water in the brook was clean and clear and Cassie remembered how her mother harvested watercress from it. The pub that she was now standing at was on a grey, dusty inner-city street, part of a terrace, the exterior unpainted for a few years. The only vegetation that could be harvested from the pub's grounds were weeds and cigarette butts. As Cassie entered the pub it was cold and dark, with a whiff of stale beer and Cassie was pleased when they were offered coffee before they started.

Despite the friendly handshake Walker had given, he looked nervous. He looked even more nervous when Cassie began by explaining that she was a Fraud Investigator with HMRC's Fraud Investigation Services, but that Winston Walker should not regard her presence there as indicating that this was a fraud investigation. She was merely present as an experienced colleague sitting in on a meeting.

Walker said he would get the coffees. Cassie asked if they could have a look around while he did so. Cassie and Jacob checked the brands of bottled beer behind the bar and they all appeared on the purchase invoices provided.

Cassie had worked with Jacob on his interview brief. The meeting had been going for about half an hour as Jacob worked through his interview brief before getting to the questions that Cassie had been waiting for.

"Have you declared all of the sales that you have made," Jacob asked Walker.

"Yes," Walker replied.

"Have you declared all of the sales that you made during the carnival?" Jacob asked.

"Yes," Walker replied again, but much slower this time.

Cassie pushed her chair away from the table and stood up. She looked at Jacob, who had taken the hint and stood up as well. Turning to Vince Abbott she said, "We will just go and sit over there while you have a word with your client".

About ten minutes later, Vince Abbott beckoned them back to the table and, once they were seated, he explained, "My client has a store room downstairs. During the carnival he set up a bar down there just selling cans. Neither the sales, nor the purchase of the cans have been included in the accounts nor the VAT returns."

Cassie looked at Walker, his head was bowed. She suggested, "Mr Walker, why don't you make us all another coffee then we can get some details about these undeclared sales."

By the time Cassie had finished her second cup of coffee they had established that this had been going on for five years. The cans cost about a pound and were sold for three pounds. On average there was about £5,000 per year in undeclared sales and the bar staff were casuals, paid cash in hand, with no PAYE operated.

All of this had been achieved because of Cassie's gut feeling and a bit of bluff, now that's what I call mentoring she thought to herself.

Criminal Investigations didn't want the case. So, Jacob would get a chance to bring the investigation to a conclusion at a further meeting with Walker. Unfortunately, unlike back in the 1980s, it wouldn't be over a pint.

About ten days later Jacob received Imran Ali's business records for his newsagent's business. Cassie wasn't at work to assist him. Jacob was quite pleased to have been able to work out how the sales figures had been arrived at from the business records provided and he had begun to prepare a business economics exercise.

Cassie had taken the day off work as her washing machine wasn't working. The repair firm said that the engineer would be there sometime between 10am and 3pm, which isn't much help when you want to work. But Cassie had lots of jobs around the house to keep her busy, including making some curtains for which she had bought the material six weeks ago. So, she decided to take the day off rather than working from home. Cassie had, of course, checked the error code that the washing machine was displaying in the user manual. The manual essentially said call an engineer. She had also rung her Dad who said, "What does the user manual say about the error code?" and, upon Cassie telling him it said ring the engineer, he said, "Well you'd better call an engineer," before unhelpfully adding, "You should've bought a Miele, the Rolls Royce of washing machines is a Miele." It was five to three in the afternoon when the engineer turned up. Cassie was having a cup of tea having finished various jobs, including the curtains. The engineer took a look at the washing machine error code and asked Cassie, "Screw or nail?"

Cassie only caught the word screw so, scowling, she did not reply to the engineer. He had, meanwhile, pulled out the washing machine and, with his head down the back of the washing machine, was oblivious to the scowl.

A few minutes later his head bobbed up again and looking at Cassie he asked, "What's that you're drinking?"

Cassie replied, "Tea".

To which the engineer said, "Don't mind if I do. Milk and two sugars please."

Ten minutes later the engineer announced he had finished and, as Cassie came into the kitchen, he held up a nail and said, "There's the culprit, a clout nail, someone has been fixing fencing panels, or a garden shed."

Cassie had visions of the previous weekend, Shaun and Barney in the garden with hammer and nails. "I'll clout them," Cassie thought.

When Cassie got in the next morning she could see that Jacob had a spreadsheet up on a screen. She asked him what he was working on. He explained he was doing a business economics exercise on Imran Ali's business records.

"Business Economics exercise on a newsagent? How many product lines have you found?" asked Cassie.

"One hundred and three," Jacob replied dejectedly.

"Let's have a look at the business records together," suggested Cassie.

Jacob and Cassie were still looking at the business records at noon, when Cassie asked Jacob, "Imran Ali only has his Newsagents business. He has declared no other taxable income and no involvement in any company or partnership that we are aware of. Is that correct?" Jacob nodded.

"Well come and look at this," Cassie gestured.

On Cassie's screen was an invoice for electricity provided to a shop in Newport called "Celebrations". Cassie googled the shop and it was a shop selling cards and gifts for every occasion. On Street View there was a big poster in the window stating, "Don't Forget Fathers' Day".

Cassie smiled at her Dad's reaction to the Fathers' Day card she had bought him last year.

"You shouldn't have bothered, Fathers' Day is an invention of the birthday card industry."

Cassie swivelled on her seat to look at Jacob and said, "We are going to pay an unannounced visit to that shop."

Cassie needed to gain authorisation for the unannounced visit which she got and she also arranged for an officer trained in downloading data to accompany them.

This turned out to be an officer called Bob. The date of the unannounced visit came and Cassie and Jacob were parked up in a car park in Newport. They then rang Bob and arranged to meet him in a local cafe. Bob was good looking and by the muscles bulging under his shirt, clearly spent a lot of time at the gym.
After a quick chat over a cup of tea to confirm the plan, the three officers made their way to the shop, putting on their HMRC ID lanyards as they entered the shop.

The shop was much like any other gift card shop. At the rear was a counter on which there was a till and a credit card reader. Behind the counter were two middle aged ladies, one in a blue blouse, the other in a red polo shirt.

Jacob approached the counter, and introduced himself to the two ladies as an officer of HMRC. He explained that this was an unannounced visit. Jacob was looking at the fact sheet in his hand so Cassie helped out.

"Which of you two ladies is in charge today?" Cassie asked.

"I suppose I am," the lady in the blue blouse replied.

Jacob took the lead again, handing the lady in the blue blouse the notice of unannounced visit and the HMRC fact sheet relating to such visits. Cassie saw out of the corner of her eye that a couple who had been browsing when she and her colleagues had arrived had now beaten a retreat and she heard the bell on the shop doorway ring as they left the shop.

Smiling at the two ladies, Cassie said, "I'm Cassie Holmes-Smith, what are your names?"

The lady in the blue blouse introduced herself as Nerys Evans and the other lady was Mavis Hopkins.

"How long have you worked here Mrs Evans?" Cassie asked.

"Four years and please call me Nerys. And you have worked here for two years now haven't you Mavis?" replied Nerys and Mavis nodded.

Cassie now moved on to the big question. "So, who do you work for, whose business is this?"

Nerys replied, "Mr Ali, Mr Imran Ali." Mavis joined in unison with Nerys with the "Mr Imran Ali" response.

Cassie couldn't help but smile.

"This is my colleague Bob," said Cassie.

"Hello Bob," Nerys smiled.

Bob took this as an invitation and, returning Nerys' smile said, "Do you mind if I download some data from the till?"

"Oh no, Cariad, you carry on," replied Nerys, still smiling Cariad being an informal term of endearment.
Cassie thought to herself, "It's a pity Bob's busy with the till, he could have asked all the questions."

Jacob had pulled out a crib sheet from his pocket and now started asking Nerys a series of questions. From which it was ascertained that the shop opened seven days a week, nine till five. There were two other members of staff, Joan Hargreaves and Jill Davies. All of the staff were paid hourly, on the national minimum wage rate. No Pay as You Earn was operated. Cash was kept overnight in a safe at the back of the unit. They used to bank the cash twice a week, but most people paid by card now so it was only banked on a Friday. Nerys had worked at the shop ever since Mr Ali began running it. It used to be a card shop run as part of one of the big gift card shop chains, but that had closed down and Mr Ali had taken over. After about twenty minutes Bob confirmed that he had downloaded all of the data, so Cassie and her colleagues left the shop.

When they got back to the office, Jacob asked Cassie, "That was fun, what do we do now?"

"Now we wait for Bob to work on the data he has downloaded. Then when we have that we can work out an estimate of the tax due and refer the case to Criminal Investigations to see if they want it," Cassie replied, and then she added, "I'm glad that you thought that that was fun because so do I."

"What, still, after all these years?" Jacob asked.

Cassie was at first a bit taken aback and then recalled that when she was in her early twenties thirty was old and forty was ancient so in reply she smiled and simply said, "Yes."

Alan had his own unannounced visit, back in the days when Tax Inspectors had their own office. An accountant, Ted Allan who had been having a meeting with one of Alan's colleagues, on passing Alan's doorway decided to see if he could convince Alan to accept that the four properties his clients, Sid Skipp, had sold should all be exempt from tax as having been his principal private residence. This was a point Alan had rejected in a long and detailed letter, not least because there was no evidence that Sid Skipp had ever lived in these properties and he had claimed exemption from council tax on the basis that the properties were unoccupied. Alan certainly was not ready to receive visitors with four Traders' files visible on his desk. He would always clear his desk before any meeting to protect the Trader's anonymity. If he was meeting with a Trader and/or their accountants he would always be smartly dressed, but right now his jacket was off, his shirtsleeves were rolled up and his tie was in his jacket pocket. He had been eating his lunch of pickled cockle sandwiches and reading the sports pages of The Times when Ted Allan carried out his unannounced visit.

Ted Allan entered the room, his eyes darting around, trying to read the files on Alan's desk. His eyes then darted to the books in the bookcase behind the desk, settling on a book Alan had placed there to be in a Trader's eyeline at a meeting which was entitled, 'How to Tell When Someone is Lying.'

From the bookcase Ted Allan's eyes darted to the sandwich and he wrinkled his nose in disgust. Only for a booming, "Yes?" to bring his eyes back to focus on Alan.

"My client Sid Skipp," Ted Allan began before pausing and then blurting out, "in your letter you imply that my client is a liar".

"So?" Alan replied, "So," said Ted Allan, picking up on Alan's response, "are you calling my client a liar?"

"Well, he told the council the properties were empty and he is telling the revenue that they weren't empty, in fact he lived in each one of them. So, he was either lying to the council then or he is lying now and my implication, as you put it, is that he is lying now."

Ted Allan had spun on his right foot and was facing the door ready to leave when he heard Alan say, "Ted?" Turning back to face Alan expectantly, he smiled at Alan, until Alan added, "Cockle sandwich?" offering the item he had noticed Ted Allan had looked at in disgust.

Ted Allan stormed from Alan's room and two days later the District Inspector (DI), received a letter of complaint about Alan from Ted Allan. The letter of complaint even complained about Alan being dressed aggressively.

When Alan was summoned to the DI's office to explain what had led to the complaint Alan asked, "What would you have said if he had barged into your office unannounced?"

The DI's chest puffed out and his eyes blazed at the mere thought of such impudence and he said, "Never mind cockle sandwiches, I'd have his balls in a bap."

CHAPTER SEVENTEEN

As Cassie was carrying out her unannounced visit Mossi was settling down in Bahrain. He had already spent time in Abu Dhabi and Qatar. As he had in the previous two locations, he spent a couple of days in a hotel to enable him time to find an apartment on a short term let.

Bahrain is an island off the coast of Saudi Arabia which sits in the Persian Gulf. Or the Arabian Gulf if you're American, as Persian Gulf would indicate it belongs to the Persians, ie, the Iranians.

If your favourite colour is beige, Bahrain is the place for you. Beige is the predominant colour. There is not a lot of green to see, apart from the sea.
It is apparently Arab tradition that the sun is so bright in Bahrain that Alah can't see. Hence, drinking alcohol and sleeping with prostitutes were permitted. Mossi's first day in Bahrain belied this as it had poured down with rain for an hour or two. Bahrain, being unused to rain, does not have any drainage system to cope with it. Therefore, lake like puddles had formed in the depressions in the road. Mossi had seen Europeans wading through the puddles the depth of a toddlers' paddling pool in a leisure centre, whilst Americans queued up to take a taxi across the puddle.

Bahrain is connected to Saudi Arabia via a causeway. Well, if you can drink alcohol and sleep with prostitutes without spending time in prison or losing part of your anatomy, it's worth building a road.

Bahrain is also home to a large US naval base and, undoubtedly, Iranian spies to keep an eye on the ships entering and leaving the harbour. If an Iranian spy wanted to know when a big carrier was coming in all he would need to do was check the naval base's cinema's upcoming schedule, if it changed from six different films a day to, say, Captain America on all screens every day, a big carrier is due in.

Bahrain's economy is primarily oil but, in recent years, it has become one of the banking centres of the Middle East. There was tourism and the Bahrain Grand Prix as well as Saudis in search of lager and ladies. A traditional trade in Bahrain, which was still an important part of the economy, was the pearl trade. This was Mossi's primary reason for visiting Bahrain, before his ultimate destination of Dubai.

As he had done in Abu Dhabi and Qatar, Mossi tended to avoid people and Westerners, as much as possible. That was with one exception, Mossi's hunt for prostitutes.

On his first night in Bahrain Mossi had heard music coming from a bar and decided to have a look. Inside he found the room full of men in traditional white Arab garb, drinking beer and watching an Arab girl, fully clothed, dancing on a stage. Whether it was because he looked Jewish or whether it was because he was wearing Western clothes Mossi felt an unwelcoming gaze from the crowd and so swiftly left.

His next stop was a bar called The Cowboy Bar. The clientele may have been Western, but they weren't wearing Stetsons and the prostitutes didn't look like the ones in Western movies either. Mossi had only taken two sips of his glass of Heineken when a girl sat down at his table and said, "Hello sugar." Her American accent was as fake as the Heineken Mossi was drinking. Fake beer was a problem in Bahrain. To avoid being sold fake beer it was best to order a Guiness, aka, Nigerian lager and Nigeria was probably a good guess as to where this prostitute came from, not that Mossi cared.

The next night Mossi found a club called Zoomers. There must have been over a hundred prostitutes in the bar and, as he squeezed his way past them to the bar, they squeezed themselves against him. Real Heineken this time and the band weren't bad either. All of the prostitutes were Chinese, none were ugly but none were what you would call pretty either. Mossi found a table and was immediately joined by two of the girls. An hour later he took them back to his hotel. Walking back to his hotel Mossi smiled as he thought to himself, "Best to have two girls as, if you have one Chinese girl, a few hours later you want another".

On his third day in Bahrain Mossi was shown a furnished apartment available for a short-term rent. The apartment was near the main hospital in the area. The estate agent showed Mossi around the apartment demonstrating the entertainment system and the cooker. Then, raving about the luxury leather sofa and the power shower, but only mentioning in passing the balcony and sea view. Mossi took the lease on the apartment and later on the balcony discovered the reason for the estate agent's reluctance to show him the sea view. There was a sea view but it was getting further away, as lorry after lorry dumped rocks and sand into the sea. Bahrain was growing literally, day by day, and Mossi could watch it happen if he wanted. Which he didn't.

That night Mossi discovered the Blue Dice Club on the seventh floor of the Hotel Riva. There was a girl on stage dancing and three other girls were sitting at individual tables, each with an Arab, each with a glass of something bubbly, but certainly not Champagne and a red rose, which even at a distance was clearly fake. Mossi liked what he saw, not the fake roses, but the girls. They were all size Zero, blonde and stunning. Mossi bought a bottle of Budweiser from the bar and sat at a table. Within a couple of minutes, he was joined by a girl who asked him if he would like to buy her a drink. Out of the corner of his eye Mossi saw another girl had appeared and was walking towards him carrying a bouquet of fake roses.

Mossi replied, "I'd like to speak to your boss." The girl disappeared and was swiftly replaced by a tall eastern European man, with dark hair and a beard. His barrel-like chest bulged under the black suit he was wearing. In stark contrast to the white traditional clothing of the Arab customers he wore a black shirt with a black tie. On his fingers were gold rings and on his wrist a gold watch. Zoltan was Hungarian, he ran these girls, all of whom were Ukrainian.

"What do you want?" Zoltan growled.

"I want to do business," Mossi replied calmly and added, "how many girls do you have?"

"Ten," said Zoltan and then said, "how many do you want?"

"All of them," Mossi replied.

With a snap of Zoltan's fingers, the frostiness was replaced by a Double Jack and Coke for both of them.

Zoltan explained that prices went up at the weekend which, in Bahrain, began on Thursday night and ended on Saturday. Mossi negotiated a price with Zoltan for the ten girls spread over the next week, which he paid up front in US Dollars. Over the next week Mossi slept with all of the girls and he selected his two favourites, Katyia and Annastasia.
Six weeks had passed by since that deal with Zoltan. Every night Katyia or Annastasia had spent the night with Mossi and sometimes both. Zoltan was happy as Mossi paid cash up front and the girls were happy because Mossi always showered before they arrived so he didn't smell of body odour like many of their punters. And he treated them well, unlike some who treated them like shit but, best of all, he would order them whatever they wanted from American Alley. American Alley was the colloquial

name of the street just outside the US naval base where you could find for sale every type of American fast food you could think of. Of course, all the fast-food outlets did deliveries. Zoltan starved the girls to keep them tiny, but a night with Mossi meant pizza, burgers, Southern Fried Chicken, whatever you wanted, all washed down with full fat Coke.

Pretty soon the girls were spending weekday afternoons with Mossi as well. They didn't usually have anything to do on these afternoons, other than get ready for the evening. Mossi had tried to keep away from places frequented by Westerners, but sometimes pleasing the girls had won out.

This week they had smoked Shisha pipes. They got some looks from the Arabs, which were equally unapproving and fascinated. They had also been go-kart racing at the go-kart race track next door to the Formula One circuit. The girls had demonstrated that size zero weight and, apparently, no fear makes a very fast go-kart driver. Today, however, they had convinced Mossi to take them to a Theme Park. Mossi sat drinking a glass of Diet Coke thinking what was more incongruous, the two size zero blondes sat to his right eating enormous bowls of ice cream, or the two women he could see in front of him who were in full Burkas, pedalling a

Pedalo at some speed across the boating lake. He took the time to consider his future plans and when to move on. He had been enjoying his time in the bedroom with Katyia and Annastasia or, to be fair, every room in his apartment but he had already spent two weeks longer in Bahrain than he had initially intended. He was starting to get bored and wanted to get back to making money instead of just spending it. The hours in the apartment dragged when he didn't have the girls to keep him entertained. Mossi had never been one to read or to sit listening to music. When he flicked on the TV, he hadn't found much to keep him tuned in. For example, camel racing, it's like a cross between greyhound racing and horse racing. Contrary to common belief, camel racing doesn't involve two bricks and a male camel's nether regions. In fact, there were actually robot jockeys concealed in the camel's saddle and, as the race is in the desert, it's in a straight line and, of course, there are no water jumps.

Camel racing looks odd on TV. But not as odd as camel beauty competitions where big pouty lips are an asset. Therefore, there is more collagen being used than in an episode of Love Island.

Mossi's eventual plan was to start a new life as David Goldman, a Dubai based, dodgy property developer, sitting on his yacht, a glass of Champagne in one hand and a beautiful woman in the other. Mossi had hoped that the beautiful woman might be persuaded to be by his side just by the attraction of the lifestyle, like the beautiful women you see on the arms of ageing Movie Directors. Or that they might be attracted to some end reward, rather than direct payment like the girls he had met holidaying in the Gambia. In the Gambia you didn't pay the girls cash, but you bought her mother a fridge freezer at the end of the week. Mossi's eyes left the boating lake and fell again on Katyia and Annastasia. They were beautiful, they would fit right in on the yacht he had planned for his new life. The girls, however, had told him they had to work for Zoltan for another six months before they could go home or move on. Mossi took another sip of his Diet Coke. Maybe he should act like a football chairman and wait until the girls become available on a free transfer under the Bosman ruling. Yes, he would give it another two weeks in Bahrain, then he would move on. If in six months' time the girls wanted to join him, all the better.

Mossi had said goodbye to the girls and to his apartment with a bit of a party. He had danced with Katya and Annastasia, the entertainment system blaring out full blast some Ukrainian disco hit the girls loved. "Who cares if the neighbours complain, I'll be on a flight out of here in three hours," Mossi had thought.

A month later Mossi, as David Goldman, had purchased a Sunseeker 64, a 47-footer. He had rented a mooring for it in one of Dubai's most desirable marinas. He had paid extra for a mooring close to the yacht club. The yacht club offered a restaurant, bars, a sauna and a pool, the costs of which were included in the annual mooring fee. The Sunseeker had cost him £600,000, paid for from his pearls and diamonds, but it was twenty years old. He had named it, "My Sea Lady", not too much of a giveaway Mossi hoped.

Mossi had initially thought of launching a crypto currency that was actually a Ponzi scheme. Paying investors their rewards with other investors' money. Such a fraud was older than Charles Ponzi, after whom such frauds had been named. Mr Myrtle, 'the man of the age,' in Charles Dickens' Little Dorrit, being a fictionalised example of such a scheme. Mossi had intended to copy the method used by the fake crypto currency One Coin whose Bulgarian founder, Ruja Ignatov, had made off with $3 billion US and whose whereabouts was still unknown. However, the more Mossi looked into the idea, the higher the start-up costs seemed to be. So, reluctantly, Mossi gave up his grand idea and decided instead to stick with his initial fraud of property development.

He didn't yet know whether to develop locally in Dubai, or back in the UK. If he was to develop in Dubai, he would need to get out more. He had been out searching for prostitutes and had found a bar called Rock Hard, with Filipino prostitutes. Mossi had even tried chatting up an attractive English woman who was in her mid-thirties who he'd seen in the gym and at the bar at the yacht club. Mossi wasn't one for great chat up lines, but, "Would you like a drink on my yacht?" had worked.

She had been unimpressed by the size and age of his 47-foot Sunseeker and had stayed just five minutes before making her excuses and leaving. Mossi was left with just a lipstick-stained Champagne flute to show for the evening and resolved from now on to stick to business and prostitutes. He thought "women like that" were only after billionaires.

Mossi met one night, a British businessman, Bruce Archibold, in the yacht club bar. They had got on well and Bruce had mentioned that he had met the captain of a super yacht at the Seaman's Mission and, through him, had learned the owner of the super yacht wanted to replace his helicopter. Bruce had managed to broker the sale of the old helicopter for a 15% commission.

Although Mossi had visions of the Seaman's Mission being some Uncle Albert looking seaman in a wooden hut, he decided to visit it that afternoon. When Mossi got out of the taxi his heart sank, there were two old boys in a wooden hut. He walked up to the hut and the more Uncle Albert looking bloke licked the end of his pencil and asked, "Ship?"

"My Sea Lady," Mossi replied.

"Name?" said the other old man.

"David Goldman," Mossi responded. An electronic lock clicked on what looked like a 7' tall garden gate. Mossi took the hint, opened the gate and walked through. Inside, much to Mossi's surprise, were swimming pools, tennis courts, a restaurant and a poolside bar. Mossi sat down at one of the stools at the poolside bar and ordered a Bacardi and Diet Coke. As Mossi was getting another drink another man sat down at the bar. His skin was red, unaccustomed to the sun, and he was sweating profusely, in some part due to the effort of carrying his 30 stone weight around.

The man turned to Mossi and introduced himself.

"Hello, I'm Dai Ginola".

"Hello," Mossi replied.

Dai Ginola continued, "I know it's a strange combination, Dai and Ginola, Welsh and French. My Dad was a French trawlerman. He used to put into Milford Haven in West Wales. My Mum worked behind the bar of The Galleon which was the nearest pub to the docks. Lazy bastard my Dad, worked hard all day but could never be bothered to walk beyond the first pub. He's dead now. We bought him a plot nearest the cemetery gate. Hah."

Dai Ginola paused, took a long sip of his whisky and ginger ale and asked Mossi, "What's your name?"

Mossi replied, "David".

Dai Ginola, meanwhile, had finished his drink and asked Mossi, "Want another?"

Mossi span on the bar stool to face Dai Ginola and replied, "Okay, Bacardi and Diet Coke."

Dai Ginola tried to spin on the bar stool as Mossi had, but 30 stones were clearly more than the spring mechanism in the bar stool could cope with. So he got off the stool and then back on facing Mossi.

Over the next four drinks Mossi learned that Dai, as Dai Ginola had insisted that he call him, was a property developer. He was currently developing an old government building on Swansea high street into student accommodation. Everything had been going smoothly when one of the workmen had cut a water pipe on one of the upper floors. This had happened one Saturday morning but the lads had to finish at lunchtime on Saturday as Wales were playing England in the Six Nations. When they had returned to work on Monday morning, everything was drenched. Dai wasn't insured, he didn't have the money to finish the development and the bank wouldn't lend him any more money. He could sell the property now and he might be able to break even but, if he had an extra million pounds to finish the development, he could make a £2 million profit.

"So, what brings you to Dubai?" asked Mossi.

"A mate of mine thought I needed cheering up and so asked me if I fancied moving a yacht from Abu Dhabi to Dubai", Dai replied.

"What are you going to do if you can't raise the extra £1 million?" Mossi enquired.

"I'll have to sell and try and break even," Dai answered.

Mossi was beginning to get interested. "There must be investors in Wales who would be willing to purchase a slice of the investment in return for a bigger slice of the profits?"

"Probably, but the ones I know I wouldn't trust and the ones that I trust aren't interested," Dai replied honestly.

"So how much of your expected profit are you willing to give up for £1 million?" Mossi asked.

Dai sipped his drink, the only sound between the two men was the sound of the ice cubes clinking together in the glass. Then Dai said, "£250,000."

"Payable when?" Mossi probed for more information on the potential deal.

"Within six months of the £1 million being paid," Dai replied, with a smile at the prospect of having found an investor and he then added, "plus 20% late interest payment per month."

"No interest," Mossi commented.

"No interest?" Dai repeated Mossi's sentence quizzically.

"If you don't pay me £1,250,000 within six months of payment, I'll kill you," Mossi said, gripping Dai's arm and looking directly into his eyes.

Seconds before Dai had been hot and sweaty, now he shivered. Looking into Mossi's eyes he had not the slightest doubt that this wasn't a threat, it was a promise. Dai knew a former nightclub owner in Swansea, Lyndon Davies, who he didn't trust not to swindle him out of the whole deal, but he didn't go round killing people. Dai convinced himself that if all went to plan, he would be £750,000 up in profit. If it didn't, he would turn to Lyndon for the £1,250,000 and he should be no worse off than if he'd gone to Lyndon in the first place. With a lot more confidence than he was feeling, Dai held out his hand and said to Mossi, "£250,000 for a six-month loan of £1 million, do we have a deal?" Mossi smiled and gripped Dai's hand as he replied, "Yes."

Mossi provided Dai with an email address he had set up in the name of David Goldman and he asked Dai to email him the paperwork relating to the property development. They swapped telephone numbers and, having drunk another round of drinks to celebrate the deal, they went their separate ways.

Back at the yacht club Mossi decided to open a bottle of Champagne. This was the life he had planned for himself, sitting on the back of his yacht in the Dubai sunshine, sipping chilled Bollinger champagne. He grasped his champagne flute, closed his eyes and closed his ears to the noise coming from a motor cruiser on his port side. The motor cruiser was larger and newer than his. It was usually quiet, but not today. Mossi tried to cut out the noise by thinking of his plans for the rest of the week. He would fly to Bahrain and sell the rest of his black pearls to raise the £1 million for Dai. He would ask Katya and Annastasia if they wanted to come and work for him fulltime.

An hour or so later the noise had died down and the motor cruiser at his port side sat silently in the water. Mossi went online and booked a flight to Bahrain the day after next which was a Tuesday.

He spent Monday on the phone to Dai Ginola and Dai's lawyers who had drawn up a contract which Mossi, as David Goldman, had signed electronically. The next day, after a short flight, Mossi arrived in Bahrain. It wasn't raining this time, instead there was a hazy sort of sunshine. So much for the sun being bright enough to blind Allah. Mossi caught a taxi to the pearl Trader's offices. The traders inspected each of the black pearls before offering Mossi his price. There followed twenty minutes or so of haggling before a price was agreed. £1 million was transferred to Dai's lawyer's escrow account and the balance of roughly £125,000 was transferred into an account in David Goldman's name. Mossi took tea with the trader to seal the deal. Mossi always found the drama of taking tea with an Arab to be greater than the taste and he was yet to see a drop spilled as the tea was poured from a great height into a small glass.

Mossi got a taxi after finishing his tea from the Trader's offices to the Jay Hotel. The shiny edifice of the hotel was located next to what the Americans would call an empty plot. Which, in Bahrain, meant a dusty area of land, which was used as an impromptu turning circle by his taxi driver. Mossi got out of the taxi and, despite it being a one-way street, looked both ways before crossing. In Bahrain it paid to expect the unexpected when crossing the road. This time was no exception as an Indian on a rusty bicycle, wearing what appeared to be his one and only T-shirt and jeans, was coming towards him, the wrong way up a one-way street, using his feet to bring the bike to a halt in the absence of functioning brakes right by Mossi. The man had a dirty carrier bag on the handle bars from which he fished out a watch and said, "Rolex? You buy?"

Mossi shook his head. The Rolex salesman, seeing the doorman from the Jay Hotel advancing towards him and, from past experience, knowing a boot in the butt would follow, pushed himself forward to get the impetus to cycle away. The doorman gave up pursuit and, instead, opened the door for Mossi. Mossi crossed the marble floor and got into the lift, selecting the seventh floor where the cocktail bar was situated. As the lift ascended Mossi wondered what a strange world it would be if someone with the money to trade in real Rolex watches would entrust their sale to a man on a rusty bike with a carrier bag. Mossi strode into the cocktail bar, took a seat on one of the bar stools and ordered a gin and tonic. The smartly dressed Filipino barmaid brought him his drink and some complimentary roasted peanuts.

Mossi got out his phone. He had three calls to make, one business and two pleasure.

His first call was to Dai Ginola, to confirm that the £1 million had been transferred.

"That's great news Butt," Dai had replied.

It took Mossi a few seconds to realise that Butt was a term of endearment, as opposed to the beginning of bad news. By the time he had realised, Dai had already rung off.

Next Mossi rang Anastasia but got the automated response that the number was no longer recognised. Mossi placed his phone on the bar, took a sip of his Gin and Tonic and popped a dry roasted peanut in his mouth.

Two Arabs entered the bar, ordered two lagers and sat at one of the tables. The Filipino barmaid took their drinks over to them together with the bill.

"Three customers now, but it's still early," she thought.

Mossi picked up his phone and rang Katiya. She answered and he asked if she would like to join him this afternoon.

Just under an hour later Katiya walked into the bar. The two Arabs who had been sitting flicking through their phones suddenly lost interest in their phones and stared at her without any embarrassment. When she sat down next to Mossi they both looked disappointed.

Mossi asked Katiya what she would like to drink.

Katiya replied, "Sex on the Beach".

A most unlikely scenario in Bahrain, due to the lack of beaches and the consequences of having sex in public on them.

"I tried ringing Anastasia, but her number was disconnected," said Mossi.

"Her brother died in the fighting, Anastasia went back for the funeral. Zoltan was furious," Katiya explained. "Anastasia waited till he was dead drunk and then crept into his room to get her passport."

"What will Zoltan do now?" Mossi asked.

Katiya replied, "Usually if a girl runs off, he would have flown out and dragged her back, but Anastasia's family lives near the front line and like me she only has a month left to work for him."

"Do you think she'll be back?" Mossi asked.

"No, she's had enough of this life," Katiya replied.

Mossi took a sip of his drink to give himself a pause before he asked, "Once your month is up, would you like to come and work for me in Dubai?"

"As what?" said Katiya, with no wish to swap life with one pimp for another.

"Shall we say my Personal Executive Assistant with particular responsibilities of keeping me happy?" smiled Mossi.

"Just you?" Katiya asked.

Mossi nodded.

"What does it pay?" Katiya said, whilst getting off her bar stool and moving closer to Mossi.

The Arabs stared again but Mossi didn't care, as he replied, "$10,000 US a month, plus the gifts a girlfriend of mine might expect.

"Well, I've seen the most wonderful handbag in the Souk, why don't you book us a cab to the Souk and a room when we get back?" Katiya answered.

The next morning, Mossi dropped Katiya off on his way to the airport. He promised to fly back to collect her in 28 days' time and fly her to a new life in Dubai. Mossi felt like the cat who had got the cream. But it was Katiya, who had got the designer handbag she had wanted, together with an offer from Mossi, that would do for now unless something better turned up.

CHAPTER EIGHTEEN

It was lunchtime and Cassie, true to her promise to Alan, had just refilled her hot water bottle. She was reading a First Tier Tax Tribunal Judgement which she had begun reading earlier in the week during her lunch break. It was a pretty straight forward judgement. The Trader who was appealing was essentially complaining that it wasn't fair to be assessed on estimated figures in HMRC's VAT assessment. The VAT assessment had been based on the best judgement of the HMRC officer.

The reason the figures were estimated was because the Trader's records had been inadvertently destroyed by him. The appeal was dismissed.

The tribunal case gave Cassie reason to recall the excuses she had heard over the years from traders:

"My accountant has them and he won't give me my records back until I pay him what I owe him."

"They were destroyed in a fire" or, "They were destroyed in a flood." But, in answer to the question, "Did you make an insurance claim?" the answer would always be, "No, I wasn't insured.

"They were stolen," but in answer to her questions such as, "What else was taken?" and "Was the theft reported to the police?" the answer would be, "Oh nothing," and "No, I didn't report the theft to the police."

Or, from a Trader running a fish and chip shop, "No, you can't have the till readings as vinegar got spilled on the till and it doesn't work anymore." Well, a VAT inspection on top of such an unfortunate spillage of vinegar, would certainly be rubbing salt into the wound.

Cassie now got out a little notebook with a, "Where's Wally?" picture on the front cover. The text of which had been altered to read, "Where's Mossi?"

"Quarter of an hour searching for Mossi and then back to work," thought Cassie.

Cassie had a gut feeling that Mossi's love of sitting on his yacht, living the life of a millionaire, would be how she would find him. So, she had been searching the websites of various marinas around the world and repeating this search periodically. She looked up in her notebook the next web address to try again and typed it in. When the website came up on the screen, she noticed that the Dubai yacht club website had a link to a new promotional film, advertising the facilities it had to offer.

She watched the film four times to check her eyes were not deceiving her before instinctively standing up and pumping her fists into the air. As her hot water bottle fell from her lap onto the floor she shouted, "Got you, you bastard!"

Alan ran to Cassie's desk. It was days later, when recollecting the moment, that Cassie thought, "I've never seen Alan run before."

Cassie pulled up Mossi's passport photo on one screen and played the film again for Alan's benefit. Alan watched the film before proclaiming, "Chummy in the background, with his eyes shut and the champagne flute in his hand, really is that bastard Mossi. Drinks are on me tomorrow, you chose where."

"The Volunteer near Cabot Circus," Cassie replied.

"I haven't been there for years," said Alan grinning from ear to ear.

After that it all happened very quickly. Cassie contacted HMRC's liaison officer with the Metropolitan Police and, within twenty minutes, was speaking to Detective Inspector Dier. DI Dier called up the film himself and Mossi's passport photo for comparison. Having seen that they were a match he said that he would email a link to the FBI and he promised to ring back later to confirm when the FBI had seen it.

For good measure Cassie also emailed the IRS a link to the website.

That was almost the end of Cassie's involvement with Mossi. The US authorities paid a visit to the marina and established that the owner of "My Sea Lady" and the man in the background of the promotional video was David Goldman. They searched, "My Sea Lady", but he wasn't on board. He was last seen wheeling a small suitcase off his motor cruiser. A check had been made of the passengers flying out from Dubai that afternoon which established that David Goldman was registered to fly on a flight to Bahrain.

Mossi had packed a small suitcase as he didn't want to rush Katiya. If he needed to spend a couple of days in Bahrain for her to sort out her arrangements before departing, so be it. She would soon be lying beside him on "My Sea Lady", soaking up the sun, as they shared a bottle of champagne.

Mossi never rushed to get off a plane. Those people who were standing up waiting to get off almost as soon as the plane had landed would probably still be waiting at the luggage carousel by the time he got there. Today, however, when he got off the plane there was still a queue of people standing in front of him, rather than the usual quick movements there would be until you got to passport control.

After about ten minutes in the queue, he could see that there was a line of five security guards checking people's passports, less than a hundred metres from the aeroplane door. Mossi felt reasonably confident that they weren't looking for him, but the nearer he got to the front of the queue the less confident he felt. When at last his turn came and he handed over his passport his right arm, with which he proffered his passport, was grasped firmly and a handcuff slapped onto his wrist. The five security guards lifted him into the air and carried him into a side room. His left arm was now twisted behind his back and the other cuff was clipped onto his left wrist. Mossi cried in pain as his arm was twisted into position. Waiting in the room were two men suited and booted. As Mossi cried, the larger of the two men spoke with an American accent.

"Does that hurt? You'll get used to that buddy. In the US, unlike you limeys, we don't send shit like you to prison as punishment, we send you to prison for punishment.

"We'll see," thought Mossi. "You don't mess with Mossi."

But, as Mossi had learned to his cost, you don't mess with Cassie Holmes-Smith either.

THE END

Printed in Great Britain
by Amazon